THEIR HARLOT BRIDE

A BRIDGEWATER BRIDES NOVEL

GOLDEN ANGEL

BRIDGEWATER
BRIDES

Cover design: Bridger Media

Cover graphic: Hot Damn Stock; DepositPhotos: Kotenko

BRIDGEWATER BRIDES

Welcome to Bridgewater, where one cowboy is never enough! *Their Harlot Bride* is published as part of the Bridgewater Brides World, which includes books by numerous authors inspired by Vanessa Vale's *USA Today* bestselling series. This is a steamy standalone read.

Enjoy!

PROLOGUE - LONDON

S *assy*

"COME HERE, YOU LITTLE WHORE," Lord Carmichael snarled, his handsome face twisted in anger as he lunged at me. My heart was racing, my mouth dry with fear. I dared not let him get his hands on me, but I also knew this could only end one way. "I bloody own you now."

"I'm not for sale!"

He laughed, a short, sharp bark of pure amusement and my cheeks flushed hot.

My *services* were for sale, just like every other woman in Mrs. Burk's House, but *I* was not. Mrs. Burk could not sell *me*. At least, that was what I told myself. She and Lord Carmichael disagreed.

"I paid for you, and now, I'll have you," he vowed, his

hazel eyes glowing hot, turning almost golden. A terrifying sight, I almost whimpered at the dangerous passion I saw reflected back at me.

The others had warned me about him when they realized he'd taken a liking to me, warned me Lord Carmichael was dangerous. His handsome features hid a mean streak. He was cruel. Obsessive. Another tart had gone with him, promised a position as his mistress after he'd paid off her debts to Mrs. Burk. She'd disappeared after leaving the house with him, never to be seen or heard from again. A month later, he'd reappeared at Mrs. Burk's, looking for another woman to bed.

What was I to do?

Mrs. Burk found me on the streets after my father died, and the landlord cast me out. I had just fled the laundry, the only place I'd been able to find work, and my hands had been chapped and bleeding. I'd been terrified after the manager had pushed me up against a wall, fumbling at my skirts. I'd fought him off and run, but I knew he'd be at me again the next day—I had no choice but to return. I needed the money.

She'd cooed over my hands, held me while I cried as I told her my sad story, and promised me I could have a better life in her house. I would have a doctor to see to my hands, a room of my own, three meals a day, and beautiful dresses. I would be safe. There would be friends.

I knew what kind of house she was taking me to, but what did it matter? The laundry manager had wanted the same thing from me. At least this way, I would have a room with a bed and a full belly, too, two things I had not had since my father died.

She had cleaned me up, brought the doctor, taught me how to please a man, then arranged for my first night with one. It had been more pleasant than working in the laundry. The other 'ladies' had been wary of me at first, but when I did not cause trouble or try to poach their callers, they had begun to relax. They warned me about several of the gentlemen who frequented Mrs. Burk's, including Lord Carmichael. I had begun to feel at home, and the work was certainly no worse than at the laundry, although I never experienced the bliss in my pussy some of the ladies claimed could happen.

Of course, there were debts. I owed her for the doctor, for my room and board, and for my dresses. She kept a strict accounting of every farthing she spent on all her ladies.

Lord Carmichael had paid that debt, and as he saw it, had transferred that debt to himself.

There was only one way this could end, and we both knew it, but I could not stop myself from trying to run from him. He was going to hurt me when he got his hands on me. It would not be the first time. Lord Carmichael liked to make women cry. The last time he'd chosen my services, I'd been left with bruises, welts, and a bite mark on my breast that had taken days to heal.

He'd had to pay extra before Mrs. Burk would let him back in the house. She'd been forced to call the doctor for me again, and I hadn't been able to work for several days.

The knowledge that she had kept him somewhat in line only terrified me more. What would he do now that he felt he owned me?

I did not want to find out.

Tears sparked the back of my eyes at the hopelessness of my situation.

"Come here, Sassy, or else you will regret it," Lord Carmichael said, almost crooning the words. The sadistic glint in his eyes told me I would regret it either way.

Still, I hesitated. The table between us was no real shield. If I ran to the door, I could not undo the lock before he caught me. I was trapped. Should I not at least try to placate him? And perhaps I could escape later...

He took advantage of my hesitation, and I screamed as he practically vaulted over the table. I turned, trying to flee, but his hand caught my long black hair, and I fell to the ground as he jerked me back, my scalp burning from the cruel pull. My hands went to my head to try to relieve the pain as tears spilled over onto my cheeks.

"Stupid cunt," he growled, his hand wrapping around my throat as he pulled me up and back against him, cutting off my air. I tried to scream, but no sound emerged. My fingers scrabbled against his, nails digging into his flesh, but his grip did not loosen. "I'm going to fuck all your holes bloody, then I'm going to take you back to my home and use you until I've had my fill. Then I'll turn you over to my men and let them have you."

Panic, already beating against my chest, turned me utterly frantic. He let go of my throat to spin me around and shove me into the table I'd been hiding behind. The edge slammed into my stomach, knocking my breath from me, my upper body flopping down across its hard surface.

Behind me, I heard fabric shift, giving me a rush of energy.

Run, run, run, run...

The word echoed in my head. I had to run. I had to get out of there. I would not meet that awful end he'd described. I would not. And I could not risk waiting to escape.

Spinning, I rolled off the table onto all fours next to the fireplace, wincing as he shouted. A hand grabbed my ankle, and I reached out, my fingers wrapping around the first thing they found—the hot poker in the fire.

He spun me around, and my arm arced in front of me, wielding the poker like a club, and he screamed when it connected with his face. Skin sizzled, and he fell back, hands to his face. The smell... God, the smell... I nearly choked on it.

Run, run, run...

A lord... I'd just attacked a *lord*. I would hang for sure if they caught me—if he didn't get to me first.

Run, run, run, run, Sassy, run, and never look back.

I scrambled to my feet, leaving the poker beside him. He was lying on his back, moaning faintly. I could see the blistered skin of his face between his fingers. Gulping, I forced myself to look away.

I had to run. But where? Anywhere I went, I would need money...

His purse.

It was by the bed, along with his coat, which he'd taken off when he first came into the room. Rushing over, I picked it up. A sick feeling roiled in my stomach. Assaulting a lord, stealing from him... I had no choice, but if I was caught...

I could not think about it.

I stuffed his purse down the front of my low-cut dress and ran to the door, hurriedly unlocking it as Lord Carmichael's groans began to grow louder. Dashing into the hall, it was blessedly empty, so I ran.

I ran down the stairs, past the startled expressions of my fellow whores and the men they were entertaining in the common room, and out the front door into the night. The shouts that followed me spurred me to run faster, and for some reason, I began to laugh, the sound slightly hysterical.

I was free.

illiam

"I CAN'T BELIEVE someone answered the ad," Clive muttered under his breath as he climbed onto the bench of their wagon and picked up the reins. I was already waiting, a small bouquet of wildflowers for our new wife on my lap. I bit my tongue against snapping back at him because I knew he didn't mean it personally. He wasn't insulting me, even though it felt that way.

I was the one who had written the ad.

I was the one who had told him someone would answer.

I was right.

Clive didn't like it when things didn't go his way. It wasn't that he didn't want a wife, we both wanted a woman in our lives, but he didn't like that my way had worked when he'd told me it wouldn't.

As much as my fingers itched to be the one driving, for once, I didn't fight him on it. He was already on edge over the woman arriving today. He couldn't control who she was, what she looked like, or what kind of wife she'd be, but he could control the horses. Over the years, I'd learned to pick my battles. Sometimes, I thought he still saw me as the scrawny teenager I'd been when he'd rescued me from the gang of men intent on stealing my week's pay.

Back then, he'd been twenty-two, four years older than me, bigger and stronger than most young men his age. With regular meals and working the ranch we shared, I'd caught up to him in weight and muscle, but he didn't seem to notice, and to be truthful, I had trouble pushing him on it. Since I owed him my life, was it really too much to let him take the lead when it was something that didn't matter much?

He was more than my partner—he was the brother I'd never had and the man I was going to share my wife with, in the Bridgewater manner. When we'd heard about Bridgewater and the way they married, two men to one woman, we'd known it was the place for us. We shared everything else, so it just made sense.

Today, I was getting my way, and our new wife was arriving. My dick was already hardening in anticipation. It had been far too long since we'd had a woman between us. I doubted any woman would be ready to jump in the middle of us immediately, but we would enjoy working her up to it and drowning her with pleasure in the meantime. When I answered him, there was no bite to my tone because I'd already won.

"There was nothing wrong with the ad. At least I didn't say she had to come with a horse like Justin and Caleb did."

Of course, somehow, they'd received an answer to their ad before we had, so the requirement hadn't set them back. I still didn't know why my ad had taken longer to find us a woman, but it had worked in the end, and that was what was important.

Clive sent me a mulish look, his dark eyes full of skepticism before he flicked the reins, getting the horses started down the lane. It felt odd to be on the wagon rather than horseback, but it made the most sense. We had no way of knowing whether or not our bride could ride, and she'd likely be arriving with luggage. It would also be easier to talk to her and get to know her a bit better if she was seated between us for the ride home.

I knew part of Clive's worry came from the unknown. Literally, everything about Miss Sassy McCloud was unknown to us except her name. I found it exciting—Clive didn't.

If she met the requirements of the ad, we'd both be happy.

Owners of the NorthWest Ranch in Bridgewater, Montana Territory, desire a wife, age eighteen to twenty-five, pretty, healthy, and able to work hard. In return, wife will be cherished and protected. No portrait necessary.

Neither of us had a preference for weight, height, hair color, eye color... we liked women. Period. Even though Clive could never be described as easygoing, I figured we could make it work with any woman sent our way if she was of the right age and constitution.

————

Clive

WILLIAM WAS GETTING that dreamy-eyed look on his face again, and I didn't know whether to sigh or smack him on the back of his fool head to knock some sense into him. The boy was a romantic and an optimist, which wasn't necessarily a bad thing but could grate on me when he ignored the realities of a situation.

Like right now.

He truly thought we were going to walk up to the train station in Travis Point and find a pretty little thing waiting for us, and we'd both fall head over heels in love with her and she with us. Then we'd get hitched in town, take her to the hotel, and pleasure her all night long.

Well... that last part didn't sound so bad, but I had no illusions about life. More likely, we were about to meet a woman with a face like a horse and the temperament of a shrew. My cock might not be able to even rise to the occasion. Sure, the other women who had come west to marry the men of Bridgewater had been fine, some of them even real pretty, but they'd had better ads.

It had taken so long for anyone to even answer William's ad, I'd begun to think no one would. I'd even been a little disappointed, although I would never tell him. I didn't think the ad had been a good idea from the beginning, but I hadn't had a better one.

The wagon rumbled along the road, passing the fields of cattle and crops as we sat in silence. I could tell he had something on his mind, but I had no inclination to ask him what. He'd speak up when he was ready.

"Don't you want a wife?" William finally asked, about a mile outside of town. He sounded a little worried. Considering the way I'd been acting, I guess I couldn't blame him.

I *did* want a wife, but one I'd picked out—*we'd* picked out together. Marrying the only woman to answer the mail-order ad seemed like a recipe for disaster, but meeting a woman around here we'd want to marry, who wasn't already claimed, would require as much luck as getting a good woman from an ad.

"I'm sure I'll feel better when I meet her," I said, which was about as cheery as I could make myself. I knew I would be much improved, even if she was a nightmare, because at least then I'd *know*. Not knowing anything was like an itch in the center of my back I couldn't reach.

The telegram she'd sent had been short and to the

point, which I would have appreciated any other time. She was coming from New York and claimed to be a hard worker, healthy, and was considered comely. Whether any of that would be true remained to be seen. Still, my heart began to beat a little faster as the wagon came closer and closer to town.

Our woman, a voice whispered in the back of my mind. *Our wife.*

A thread of excitement trickled through me, even as I tried to push it back. There was no point in getting excited until we saw her... and she saw us. Hell, she might not even want us once she realized it was an 'us.'

William thought his ad had made it clear *we* were looking for a wife, but outside of this territory, who would believe such a thing?

―――

SASSY

I SPREAD the ad and the last telegram over my lap, re-reading the small scrap of paper over and over again.

Will meet you at the train station in Travis Point. Will have flowers for you. – William

Knowing how to look for him made me feel a bit easier, but only a bit. I glanced out the window to the golden fields rolling by. So open and empty, they went on for miles, making me feel even smaller than I already did.

How could someone hide when there was nothing to hide behind? It was nothing like London or New York City, nothing like anything I'd ever known. I had to hope the difference and the many miles would be enough to keep me safe.

Heavy boots tramped down the train aisle, and I flinched, ducking my head as the man passed by my bench seat. He wouldn't have been able to see anything, anyway. I had tucked myself between the window and a large woman who was both taller and broader, and I was still wearing my bonnet to hide my face.

My fingers shook as I looked down at the ad again.

Protected.

That had been the word I'd responded to. I wanted to feel safe again, even if I had to cross an ocean and go all the way to the Montana Territory to do it.

New York City hadn't been safe. Lord Carmichael's money got me there, and I'd found a job sewing in a factory until I decided my next move. I hadn't dared ply my former trade. Part of me hoped Lord Carmichael might forget about me, but when I remembered his screams, the blood on his face, and the smell of his burned flesh, I knew I couldn't trust that hope. For a man like him, I doubted an ocean could keep me from his vengeance. From the first, I'd known the city would be the very first place he'd look for me, so my only hope was to disappear.

Overhearing the other women in the factory, talking about men looking for brides out west, giggling as they read the ads in the paper, spurred me to look, too. A woman could disappear out west, couldn't she?

William's last telegram hadn't come too soon.

The day it arrived, one of the women at the factory told me some men were asking about a woman of my description with a British accent.

"But they're looking for a whore." Penny had giggled, sincerely amused. "Not someone as buttoned-up as you are."

Somehow, I'd managed to laugh, even as panic clawed its way up my chest. I'd gone straight home to the boarding house after work that night, snuck in the back door, and cleared out my room. It was already paid up through the week, so I didn't feel any guilt about my abrupt departure.

I used the last of Lord Carmichael's money to buy myself a few new bonnets, my train ticket, and a hotel room to stay in until my train departed. Hiding my face and hair with the deep bonnets, I spoke as little as possible, doing my best to ape an American accent when I did. People looked at me oddly, but as long as I didn't sound British, I didn't care.

It wasn't until I finally stepped on the train, I was able to breathe easier, the tightness around my chest finally loosening. Tracking me to New York was no hard feat, especially since I was likely remembered on London's docks—I hadn't been thinking about hiding myself then —but surely, he wouldn't be able to follow me west. Even if he did, I'd have a husband to protect me. Cherish me.

That was what the ad had promised. I wanted to be cherished. To fall in love. To feel my body come alive with a man. I had been told it was possible, despite my experiences. Perhaps I had no right to be hopeful for such a thing, but I hoped all the same.

The train began to slow, and my heart bounced inside my chest as my head jerked up to look out the window at the town rolling into view. Off in the distance, there were mountains standing between the land and the blue of the sky, looking smaller than I'd imagined they would be. Perhaps they were bigger when one got closer.

There were no large buildings or bustling streets, although there were people milling about. There was something strange about the scene, and it took me a moment to realize what I found odd—there was no one rushing about, no one seemed to be in a hurry.

The conductor came by, shouting for all the passengers who were going to Travis Point and Bridgewater. The woman beside me snorted and came awake as I pulled my suitcase down from the shelf above us.

"You're getting off here?" she asked, sounding shocked and a little scandalized.

I frowned. "Yes..."

She eyed my attire, which covered me completely. Penny had called me "buttoned-up" for a reason. It didn't always keep the men at bay, unfortunately, but it helped a little.

"Wouldn't have figured you for a harlot."

Shocked, I stared at her, then the conductor was

yelling again, and I had to hurry to get off the train. The word echoed in my mind. Why had she called me that? I didn't have time to ponder the mystery, though. Almost as soon as I stepped off the train, I saw the man I was to meet.

There weren't many people about, which made it very easy to see the two men on the far side, one of them holding a small bouquet of pink, white, and blue flowers —the only one on the platform holding flowers.

My lips parted in surprise.

I didn't know what I had been expecting, but I knew it wasn't this. Both men were tall and broad-shouldered, although William was a little shorter than the man beside him. He had a wide smile on his clean-shaven, handsome face that instantly made me want to like and trust him, a rather scary feeling after not being able to trust anyone for so long. The man standing next to him was handsome despite his scowl, his face scruffier than William's but still quite striking.

To my surprise, something in my body stirred as I looked at them. Something I had only felt a few times before when one of my customers had been more attentive than usual—a little ache inside. I was *aroused*. The shock of it held me still for a moment before I managed to shake it off and approach them, quaking from both fear and my body's reaction.

illiam

Looking at the few people coming off the train, I knew the moment I saw her, I was looking at our wife. She was the only woman traveling alone. My body reacted, my cock thickening at the very sight of her. It didn't matter that her dress had sleeves to the wrist and was buttoned all the way to her throat, or that her hair and face were completely hidden by her dark green bonnet. I could see the grace in her movements, her neat waist, and the generous curves of her body, and I wanted her.

When she approached and finally lifted her head, so I could see her face, my breath caught, and I nearly choked.

"William West?" The soft lilt of her voice had an

accent I recognized from some of the soldiers who had made their home in Bridgewater, but I scarcely paid attention to that as she put her bag down and stood before us.

Considered comely.

That's what her first telegram said. I had hoped for fair enough to be attractive to both Clive and me, but I never expected *this*. Beside me, Clive cursed under his breath, low enough, even I couldn't hear exactly what he said, but it didn't matter. I stared back at our soon-to-be-wife, transfixed.

Skin that looked sun-kissed—likely her natural coloring if she wore bonnets like that all that time—a heart-shaped face, finely pointed dark brows over wide black eyes, a man could fall into and drown. Her lips were a dark pink pout, plush and full, the kind of lips a man wanted to see wrapped around his cock.

Wrapped around *my* cock, which had hardened so fast, I felt almost dizzy from the need pounding through me.

Her eyebrows began to furrow, and I realized I hadn't answered her. Clearing my throat, I thrust the flowers in my hand at her.

"That's me. Sorry... I just... you're beautiful."

"Thank you," she said, but her smile didn't quite reach her eyes, which made me wonder. A woman on her own, who looked like she did, probably garnered unwanted attention, which explained the deep bonnet.

Protectiveness welled up inside me. She tilted her head at Clive. "Hello. I'm Sassy McCloud."

"Sorry," I said, jumping in as I realized my mistake. "This is Clive North, my partner and your other husband-to-be."

Sassy's eyes widened in alarm, and the hand she'd started to hold out was snatched back.

"Other..." Her voice trailed off faintly.

"Told you this was going to happen," Clive scoffed and looked at me. I could tell from his expression, he was just as attracted to her as I was, but that didn't stop him from being his usual grumpy self.

I glared at him before turning back to Sassy.

"The ad said we were looking for a wife. Bridgewater is known for having a different way of marriage. The founders of the town decided they wanted a place where they could follow Mohamiram customs and settled here. We mostly marry two men to one woman."

I pointed at the town, where several triads walked down the town's only thoroughfare. Sassy's head turned, the wide brim of the bonnet blocking my view, so I couldn't see her expression as she examined them. I paused, giving her a moment to take it in, but of course, Clive had to comment.

"If that's a problem, speak now or forever hold your peace."

I wanted to groan. His terrible sense of humor raised itself at the oddest times. I was pretty sure he thought we were about to be rejected and wanted to hurry the process along.

"Legally, you'll only be married to me," I said hurriedly. "But both Clive and I will both act as your husbands. If you'll have us."

I held my breath for her answer.

———

SASSY

TWO HUSBANDS.

Impossible.

Yet... I didn't think they were lying or joking. As I watched, one of the women in the street kissed both the men she was with on the lips before going into a store. The two men stood outside, fondly watching her go before turning to talk to each other once she was inside.

That strange little curl of arousal began to ache a little bit more. Why my body was reacting this way, I didn't know. I had never experienced it outside of a man actually touching me, yet neither of these men had laid a finger on me.

But they were both going to.

A shiver went down my spine.

"If I say it's a problem?" I asked, curious about their answer. Neither man set off a sense of danger, other than my odd reaction to them, but I was still in shock at the idea of having two husbands rather than one. I thought the ad meant they were both looking for their own wife, not the same one.

The comment from the woman on the train suddenly made sense. She must have known Bridgewater's reputation.

"Then we'll invite you to stay and get to know us a bit before you make a decision," William said. Clive's expression didn't change, but an air of disapproval hung around him all the same. Strangely, that didn't deter me. I'd rather know what he was feeling. William smiled reassuringly. "Don't worry, sweetheart. We'll be gentle with you. Your wedding night won't be anything but pleasure."

Heat flushed my cheeks, and I bit my lip as I realized their assumption about my hesitation. From the beginning, I'd decided to hide my past employment. Everyone treated whores differently. Likely, they assumed I was a virgin. My extremely modest attire was to help disguise myself, but it was also the reason Penny had called me "buttoned-up" and had thought I was a prude. I had been so focused on reaching safety, I had barely given thought how I would handle my non-virgin status.

Harlot.

The woman's comment drifted through my mind. Perhaps my experience would be an asset... but no, I dare not risk it. They would likely turn on me, and if they told anyone about my former occupation, it would make it easier for Lord Carmichael to find me. While I hoped I'd fled far enough, he would cease his efforts, I would not risk assuming that.

I would have to pretend to be the virgin I was once; that's all there was to it. I would not make them wait, either. I needed protection, and men would be more protective of a wife than of the woman who *might* become one. If I were completely honest, I was also curious about my body's reaction to them. I was attracted to them, both of them, in a way I'd never felt toward any other man. I could not help but wonder if that would make a difference when they bedded me.

Straightening my spine, I nodded my head. "I will marry you. Both of you."

———

Clive

"WHY?" I asked suspiciously before William could jump on her acceptance like the eager puppy he resembled. He was practically wagging his tail and had been since we got our first good look at Miss Sassy McCloud—not that I could blame him.

She was stunningly beautiful, the kind of beauty that turned heads and made it impossible for people to forget her. She was aware of it, too, or she wouldn't be hiding her face. It made me wonder what else she was hiding. There had to be something. What sent a woman who looked like *that* this far west for a husband? Surely, she hadn't lacked for suitors where she came from.

My cock was hard as a rock, just looking at her and imagining stripping her of those prim clothes, so we could make her scream with pleasure.

She blinked, her long lashes sweeping over her cheeks.

"That's what I came here to do, isn't it? Get married? If two husbands are the custom of your town, I have no objection. I would rather two husbands than none at all."

William started to open his mouth, but I held up my hand to stop him. I could practically hear his teeth grinding in frustration, but he didn't intervene with my questioning. We *both* had to agree to marry her.

"How is it a woman as beautiful as you couldn't find a husband before now?" I asked, glaring down at her.

She paled a touch, gulping, and her gaze dropped along with her voice, which became little more than a whisper. "There... there was man..."

Fear. That's what I heard in the tremble of her voice, and a fierce protective instinct rose inside me, batting aside both my suspicion and my arousal.

"A man you didn't want to marry?" William asked gently, reaching out to take her hand. She hesitated but put her fingers in his, nodding.

"H-he was very angry when I rejected him. And... he is a very powerful man. H-he did not want to *marry* me." She bit her plush lower lip as anger on my behalf began to rise inside my chest. "I wanted to be far enough away, he would not, could not follow. I... perhaps this was a mistake. I do not want to bring trouble to anyone else. I just want to be safe." Sincerity rang in every word she spoke.

So, she was running from a man she didn't want, and it sounded as though he'd made her a dishonorable offer. I relaxed, although I still wished the man in question was in front of me, so I could teach him a lesson about how to treat a woman. William and I exchanged looks.

"We'll keep you safe," William said reassuringly. He was better at sweet talking than me. "You'll be completely safe as our wife."

Sassy's head tipped back, and she peeked at me from underneath her bonnet. I nodded firmly.

"However much power he has back east, he doesn't have any here. You don't have to marry us, though. We can keep you safe, regardless."

I wasn't going to let any woman go unprotected. William glared at me, but then his expression softened, and he nodded, squeezing her hand as he realized what I meant.

"Clive's right. You don't have to marry us unless you truly want to."

"I want to," she said hurriedly. "I-I want to be a wife. And I find you, both of you, very, um, handsome." She blushed a very charming color of pink.

William preened at her words. I couldn't help but straighten up a touch myself. She was attracted to us. What man wouldn't enjoy hearing that?

"Well, then, let's get to the church, sweetheart," William said, lifting her hand to his lips, giving it a kiss before he bent down to take her luggage from her. She only had the one case, which he hefted easily.

Placing my hand on the small of her back, I felt a slight tremble run through her as William and I flanked her, guiding her off the platform toward the church where the preacher would be waiting.

———

SASSY

PLEASE, oh please, don't let this be a mistake.

That was the only thought running through my mind as I pledged to love, honor, and obey my husbands. Any doubts that they were jesting about both of them marrying me fled once we were standing in front of the preacher, who immediately told them both to take my hands. It was a strange custom, but perhaps a very good one for my circumstances.

Two husbands to protect me.

Two husbands to please.

Fortunately, I was well versed in pleasing more than one man a day.

Two husbands to protect me.

I still felt a touch of guilt about misrepresenting what Lord Carmichael had wanted from me, but when

William had made the suggestion, I had gratefully latched onto it. Running from an unwanted marriage sounded much better than running from a man who thought he owned me because he'd paid my debts to the brothel where I'd worked.

"I now pronounce you husbands and wife," the preacher said, pulling me out of my thoughts and back to the ceremony, binding me to Clive and William. "You may kiss the bride."

William turned to face me, pulling me into his arms for a kiss. It started sweetly, a gentle press of his lips against mine, and my heart fluttered in my chest as a warm wave of arousal washed over me. My nipples tingled, hardening against his broad chest as his hands pressed against my back. The kiss deepened, his tongue sliding into my mouth, coaxing a response from me, and I sighed against his lips, melting against him.

Then the kiss was over, and William spun me back around to face Clive. My senses already humming, I gasped as Clive took hold of me and claimed my mouth. That was what it was—not a kiss, but a statement. Unlike William, Clive wasn't gentle, but my body responded all the same. The contrast between the two of them aroused me even more.

I felt the heat of William's body against my back, pressing into me, and I whimpered as Clive's tongue invaded my mouth, his hand on the back of my neck, holding me in place. When he let me go, I was breathless and panting. Between the two of them, my body was stirred up in a manner no man had ever achieved before. Oh my... what had I gotten myself into?

"Let's head to the hotel," Clive said, hand settling on the small of my back again as William's fingers closed around mine. "We can have dinner before we got upstairs for the night."

"If that's alright, Sassy?" William asked, his blue eyes glinting with hope.

My legs felt a little unsteady as they guided me forward, William stooping to pick up my suitcase again with his free hand.

"That's... that's fine," I managed to say through lips still tingling from the impact of their kisses.

"Good luck!" The preacher called as we exited the church. I appreciated the sentiment—I had a feeling I was going to need it.

 *illiam*

DINNER PASSED QUICKLY. Sassy had been a bit overcome by our kisses, but she'd recovered by the time we reached the hotel. She wanted to know all about the ranch and what we expected from her as a wife. As usual, I did most of the talking with Clive interjecting here and there.

We wanted her to be able to cook, clean the house, keep our clothes mended, and—eventually—take care of any children who came along. Of course, we'd help with all of those as we were able, especially the children, but ranching was long, hard hours. She'd be in charge, for most of it. Of course, thinking about eventual children reminded me how much I wanted to start practicing having them with our new wife.

Clive couldn't take his eyes off of her, either. As soon as she'd admitted she was running from something, I knew he'd be in agreement. More than anything, Clive was a protector—always had been. Gruff as hell on the outside, he had a soft, squishy heart that couldn't bear to see someone in trouble without wanting to help them.

As we finished our meal, Sassy became more and more nervous, fidgeting in her seat, her gaze flicking back and forth between us. Clive was looking at as if she was a dessert, he wanted to sink his teeth into, and I didn't think I was doing much better. Both of us were looking forward to our wedding night.

"Well, then," I said, looking around at our empty plates. I cocked my head at Sassy. "Ready to go upstairs?"

Nervous but not frightened was how I interpreted her nod. We led her to our room, which we'd stopped at earlier to leave her case. Once inside, she stood awkwardly in the center of the rug, nibbling on her lower lip, and peeking at Clive and me as though she wasn't sure where to look.

"It's okay, sweetheart," I said, stepping forward and gently pulling her to me. Her head tipped back, dark eyes widening when her lower body came into contact with mine, the hard ridge of my dick pressing against her soft stomach. "We'll go slowly. I'll be gentle."

I lowered my mouth to hers, taking another kiss, while Clive moved around behind her and started taking the pins out of the coils of her dark hair. Sassy slowly relaxed as I coaxed her lips open, kissing her more thoroughly. Hair brushed against my fingers, where they fell on her back—Clive had pulled all the pins out. The soft strands were like black silk, whispering across my skin.

She moaned a little, and I glanced up to see that Clive was massaging her scalp.

"That's good, Sassy," Clive said, his voice deep and rough. "You just relax. William and I are going to take care of you."

My cock jerked. Hell yeah, we were—in every way possible.

She squirmed against me, the way a woman does when she's aroused, and I took that as a sign to deepen the kiss. My cock dug into her belly, throbbing and aching to be inside her, but I knew we had to take our time. Ease her into things. She had two husbands to take care of, so we needed to be gentle with her.

Her hands were on my chest, fingers flexing against me as I kissed her and kissed her. When I pulled away, her eyes were slightly glazed, and the look of surprise on her expression nearly made me grin.

"Such a pretty wife," I said, rubbing her hips as Clive pressed against her, his hands sliding from her back to her front, cupping her breasts from beneath and making her gasp. "We want to touch you and make you feel good all over."

"Oh, my..." Panting for breath, she closed her eyes as I undid the buttons down the front of her dress, right through the center of Clive's hands as he massaged and squeezed her breasts. The light tan of her skin was visible through her chemise and went all the way down to where her corset started, confirming it was her natural coloring.

Working together, we slid her dress off, and Clive spun her around, taking his turn to kiss her while I pulled the laces of her corset loose. We took turns taking her mouth, spinning her back and forth between us while we undressed her, keeping her too dizzy to be shy.

———

Sassy

HEAT BLOOMED INSIDE MY BODY, befuddling my senses. The two men were taking their time undressing me, and it felt almost odd to be naked in front of men again—odd but comfortably familiar. This was something I knew how to do, even if it had been a long time.

"So beautiful," Clive said, staring down at my breasts with their dark pink nipples. The little buds were stiff and aching from the caresses he and William had bestowed on them as they'd undressed me. My whole body was aching. Needy. Was I finally going to experience the bliss the other women at Mrs. Burk's had talked about? It felt like it. I was wet between my legs, so very wet, throbbing, and needy.

For the first time ever, I truly wanted a man inside me.

No, not just *a* man—one of *my* men, one of *my* husbands.

Before, I would not have thought there was much difference between men, but right now, I wanted them and no one else.

As they passed me back and forth, they'd been undressing as well, stripping off their garments when it wasn't their turn to kiss me, but I had been too distracted to notice until William scooped me up in his arms and carried me to the bed, with Clive following. They were both nicely muscled, broad-shouldered, and had hair curling on their chests. Clive had more than William—or perhaps William's hair was just less noticeable because it was lighter.

They both had long, thick cocks, and Clive's fingers wrapped around his, fisting it. My eyes widened when I realized he was watching me watch him, but he did not seem to mind.

"Get her on her back," he ordered William.

"Don't—" I cut myself off, horrified at what I'd almost revealed.

"Don't worry," Clive said, chuckling as he stroked his cock. "You'll like this, sweetheart."

I did not know what he planned, but I was mortified. I had almost told him not to forget a French letter. I was so used to doing so at Mrs. Burk's, it had nearly slipped out, but there would be no French letters or vinegar sponges here. Likely, they wanted me pregnant, and I doubted they were worried about the pox as we'd had to be.

————

Clive

OUR WIFE WAS BEAUTIFUL. The clothing hadn't been able to hide that, but it had tempered some of the effect. Now that she was naked, every inch of her visible to our hungry eyes, we could truly appreciate how stunning she was. She was deliciously curved, lightly tanned head to toe, with dark pink nipples, a thatch of black curls over her mound, and pretty, dark pink lips just beneath them.

William sat down on the bed, spreading his legs, so he could settle her between them, her back against his front, leaving her facing me. Sassy's hands fluttered in front of her as if she couldn't figure out where to put them. William slid his hands down her arms to her wrists, drawing them up and back to loop around the back of his neck.

"Keep your hands right here, sweetheart," he murmured in her ear as I crawled onto the bed, still pumping my cock.

"We're going to make you feel so good," I told her, letting go of my cock to spread her legs wide apart. With her hands behind William's neck, her breasts were thrust up, and her body was completely open to us both. The expression on her face was somewhat dubious, and I almost chuckled.

"Do you know how a man makes love to his wife?" William asked, his hands sliding over her stomach, then up to her breasts. She gasped when he cupped the soft mounds, pinching her nipples lightly.

"I... yes?" It was more of a question than an answer. "I... the other women in the factory I worked in... they'd talk sometimes..."

I bent my head, kissing her leg, and she gasped, her leg jerking in response. Placing my hands on the inside of her knees, I spread her legs wider, holding them in place as I kissed up the inside of her thighs. Sassy whimpered, squirming slightly, but unable to move in her current position. My cock pressed against the mattress beneath me, which felt good, but not as good as it would once I sank inside her. That would have to wait a bit, though.

"Did they tell you it could feel good?" William asked, rolling her nipples between his fingers.

"Y-yes..." She sounded a little dubious, and this time, I did chuckle.

Picking her legs up, I draped them over William's thighs, completely opening her pussy to me. The dark fringe of curls provided a lacy frame for the swollen lips, the mauve interior glossy with her arousal. She was fucking perfect, and she was all ours.

"Just hold on to William," I said, glancing up at her and meeting her startled gaze. "I'm going to show you just how good it can feel."

Lowering my head down between her thighs, I pressed my mouth against her wet softness and began to feast.

SASSY

"OH, GOD!" I nearly levitated off the bed, every muscle in my body tensing with shock as Clive put his mouth on me, his tongue lapping at my sensitive flesh. I'd used my mouth on a man before, of course, but I'd never been the recipient. I hadn't minded the lack as it seemed like it would be extremely intimate, and I hadn't wanted that.

Now, I knew it was *extremely* intimate. Clive's face was buried between my thighs, and he was tasting me, savoring me. William's hands played with my breasts and nipples, his lips moving along the side of my neck. Both of them were fully involved in giving me pleasure without taking any for themselves.

It was confusing beyond belief. Nothing I had ever experienced prepared me for this.

I knew they wanted me. Clive had been stroking his cock, and I could still feel William's rod pressing against my spine, hard and ready, yet their focus remained on me.

If I had been in a different position, I would have tried to reciprocate, but with my arms above my head with my hands wound about William's neck, there was nothing I could do except squirm on his lap as he fondled me, and Clive licked and sucked my most sensitive parts.

I moaned, arching as Clive's tongue laved over a

shockingly sensitive area, then I felt a finger press inside me. Clenching around the invasion, small though it was, my body reacted the way it had been trained.

"Mmmm... nice and tight," Clive murmured before sucking on a part of me that made me cry out as pleasure surged through me. His finger pumped, and I spasmed around the questing digit.

"Oh, please..." The needy ache was becoming unbearable, like an itch, I couldn't scratch but so much more encompassing and so much worse. William's fingers pinched my nipples harder, adding a little bite to my growing pleasure and making me feel even more frantic. "I need... I need..."

"We know what you need," William growled in my ear. "Just relax, sweetheart. Clive's going to make you come for us."

Another finger joined the first, sliding between my folds, then the hot suction of Clive's mouth clamped down. The need inside me burst like a dam breaking open, and I screamed with both shock and pleasure at the ecstasy that billowed across my body. The men held me, William's fingers tugging, Clive's lips pulling as I held onto William for dear life, buffeted back and forth by the intense rapture. Every part of my body was tingling and buzzing, my insides spasming, and I was nearly senseless from the cascade of sensations. My muscles went lax, and I panted, out of breath and dazed.

I hadn't known it could feel like that.

Then Clive's mouth left me, and he knelt between my thighs.

I only had a moment for fear and nerves to grip me, worrying he would know something was wrong, then he was groaning as he slid his thick, hot, hard cock inside me. Clamping down around him, I squeezed tightly. I was exquisitely sensitive, but the stretch of my muscles opening for him actually felt good.

It didn't hurt at all, shocking me.

"Feels so damn good," he gritted through his teeth, pulling his hips away, then thrusting forward, sliding deeper. William's hands tightened on my breasts, and I could feel him staring over my shoulder, watching as Clive buried his cock in my quivering sheathe. Knowing he was watching added a layer of unexpected eroticism. I would have never guessed I would like being watched, but right now, it aroused me even more.

Bottoming out, Clive held himself for a moment, then thrust hard, several times, making me cry out as his flesh rubbed against mine. It didn't hurt, not at all, but the sensations were so intense against my hypersensitive flesh, I couldn't stay quiet.

When he pulled out, I nearly panicked, worried he had taken my cries the wrong way and would be disappointed.

"I'm fine! I'm sorry, I'm fine!"

"Shh, shh, it's fine, sweetheart," he said, his lustful gaze softening as he pulled me onto his lap, spinning me around, so he was holding me the same way William had been. "William and I agreed—I'd have you first, but he'd come inside you first."

"Trust me, sweetheart, you don't have anything to be sorry about." William grinned, his eyes alight as he crawled toward me. It was his turn to drape my legs over Clive's thighs, opening me up as he knelt between them, cock gripped in one hand. He slid it up and down my wet center, coating the head with my arousal. He groaned. "Fuck, she's so wet."

"Yes, she is," Clive murmured, fondling my breasts, the way William had but a little rougher. The tiny bite of pain as he pinched and rolled my nipples made me squirm, reigniting the needy ache inside of me, I thought had been satisfied by his mouth. "Go on, then, William. I want to watch you make our wife come a second time."

With another groan at Clive's words, as if he was already imagining it, William pressed forward, burying himself in my pussy, and I moaned as he filled me.

For the first time, I wondered marriage might be more than I could handle.

4

 *illiam*

WATCHING Clive sink into our wife had been hot as hell.

Sinking into her myself was even better.

Soft, wet heat surrounded my cock, and Sassy gasped as I groaned. As her pussy clamped down around me, she arched. Clive's hands played roughly with her breasts, pinching her little nipples harder than I had while his teeth dragged over the side of her throat. Watching them made it even harder for me not to lose myself in her, but I didn't want to hurt her.

We wanted to make sure our wife knew, having two men in her bed wasn't going to be a hardship. She'd still likely be sore after this first time, but hopefully, she'd feel good. The lack of blood was a relief—her maiden barrier must have been easily breached, which I would think meant she'd recover more easily.

I thrust, slow, smooth strokes while she wriggled and moaned, panting for breath as we pleasured her. My balls ached as I moved inside her, the slick cradle of her body, squeezing the full length of my cock every time I filled her. Despite the orgasm she'd had on Clive's lips, I was determined to make her come for me as well, and I could feel her starting to respond to me already.

I wanted to feel her spasming around my cock.

"That's it, good girl," I crooned, my hand sliding up her thigh to rest on her mound, my thumb dipping down between our bodies to caress her clit.

"Oh!" She jerked when I touched the slippery nub, her eyelashes fluttering rapidly. My thumb circled, my hips slowing, so I could touch her more easily. Clive grinned, watching her writhe for us. "Oh, God…"

I began to move a little harder, a little faster, circling her clit the whole time. Her eyes widened in shock, and she stared down between our bodies. Propped up against Clive, she could see my cock, glistening with her arousal, pushing in and out just under where my thumb was manipulating her sensitive flesh. It was a sight worth seeing.

Clive tugged on her nipples, and she whimpered, eyelashes fluttering again, and her head dropped back against his shoulder. Her pussy spasmed around me, squeezing my cock and sending delicious sensations up and down my spine.

Our beautiful wife was about to cream herself all over my cock.

————

Sassy

I CRIED out as ecstasy washed over me again, William's cock plunging relentlessly, his thumb rubbing that oh-so-sensitive nub and sending waves of bliss through my body. His hot eyes devoured me, looking at me as though I was a goddess.

I felt like one.

William's hands moved to my hips, thrusting harder, more roughly. I whimpered as my sensitive flesh shuddered around his cock as every thrust pressed his body against my little button of pleasure. Gasping and writhing, my pleasure went on and on.

I felt him shove deep, pulsing, and for the first time, I felt the hot spurt of his cum. My pussy clenched around him, and I shuddered at the sensation of him throbbing against the walls of my body. Panting for breath, I went limp against Clive.

Clive was murmuring in my ear, whispering what a good girl I was as his hands caressed me, his cock digging into my back. Atop me, William's head hung down, and he dropped a smattering of kisses on my shoulder.

I had never felt like this with any other man.

So cared for. So attended to. So satisfied.

I had been told it could feel this good but had never experienced it.

Rolling off, William laid on his side beside me, his eyes glowing with approval. I smiled back at him, happy to have pleased him.

"Think you can handle one more husband?" Clive asked, slipping out from beneath me.

My head dropped back against the mattress—a much more familiar position, even if it had been months. My legs were still spread, and I felt muzzy, satiated... but I did not want to disappoint either of my new husbands.

"Yes," I said immediately. William smiled. Clive studied my face intently, as though he suspected I wasn't telling the truth. I bit my lip. Should I have said no? Would a virgin have said no?

"I won't be mad if you want to wait," Clive said, his fingers stroking my inner thigh, then up to my swollen pussy. I moaned as he touched the soft, swollen folds. Not because I was aroused again, but because I was so incredibly sensitive, even that soft touch elicited a reaction. "You're likely to be sore tomorrow, as it is."

I hesitated only a moment, but I told the truth. "I still want to... consummate my marriage with both of my husbands."

Not because I thought it would bind them to me, although there was that as well. I truly wanted to please Clive. I didn't need another climax, but I wanted the intimacy and wanted to feel claimed by both of the men who had married me.

Clive's eyes burned so hot, I felt seared by his gaze, then his mouth came down hungrily on mine, his body wedging between my thighs. I whimpered when I felt his hard cock nudging at my pussy. He ended the kiss, pulling back, so he could settle his cock in the right spot. I was extra slick, thanks to William, when Clive thrust in hard and fast, making me cry out as my body was opened again.

"Good girl," William murmured, leaning in to kiss me as Clive began to thrust. "Just relax. We're going to make you feel so good again."

Again?

Not possible.

But as William's lips moved over mine, his hand sliding across my skin to palm my breasts, I could feel a tingle stirring deep inside. What were these men doing to me, and how?

Clive was rougher than William, moving faster and harder, but my body welcomed it. I was too sensitive for slow movements, which would have dragged against my tender flesh.

Hooking my legs into his elbows, Clive leaned forward, his body rubbing against my swollen nub every time he buried himself. I cried out as little quakes of pleasure shook me, feeling as if my climax hadn't really ended, as if the fire hadn't quite gone out, and now, the embers fanned to new flames.

I didn't know if I could take any more pleasure, but I wasn't going to have a choice.

William held my hands as Clive plowed into my pussy, and the flames of rapture licked through my body. I was brimming with bliss, overflowing with ecstasy as Clive's hard cock impaled me, filling me completely, and I spasmed around him.

Even before his weight came down, I had gone limp and nearly insensible from the overload of pleasure.

———

Clive

PANTING AND SPENT, I braced myself against the bed to keep my full weight from falling on Sassy. It felt as if I'd emptied every drop of energy into her willing body, all the pent-up tension gone from my muscles, which were now a bit wobbly. Lowering my forehead, I gently brushed my lips over hers before pulling away. When my cock slid from her body, she whimpered.

"Our beautiful wife," William said, leaning over to give her a kiss as well.

Sassy blinked up at us, her eyelids clearly growing heavy.

"Thank you," she whispered, her eyes closing.

"For what?" I asked, but she didn't answer. William and I exchanged a bemused glance, but it was clear she was already falling asleep. Between her long train ride and then taking care of two lusty husbands, it wasn't surprising she was tuckered out. I couldn't remember a time when a woman had ever thanked us before, although I supposed the sentiment wasn't inappropriate.

Maybe she was thanking us for being gentle with her. I'd heard stories about wedding nights where things went terribly wrong, perhaps she had, too. We'd been so gentle with her, she hadn't even bled, even though I'd been aching to take her hard after I'd first slid into her. Or maybe she was thanking us because we'd married her? She certainly didn't seem afraid anymore.

Kissing her shoulder, I pushed myself up and looked down at the pretty picture she made.

Her thighs were still spread, knees falling to the sides, nipples and pussy dark pink from use. Mine and William's combined seed was already starting to seep from her body, a trickle of white against her dark curls.

Calling her beautiful almost didn't do her justice. She was gorgeous and ours... all ours. The level of possessiveness I felt looking at her was unnerving. I barely knew her, and I would already do anything to keep her safe. I liked to think that was true about any woman, but Sassy had already become monumentally more important to me than anyone else—even Will. From the adoration on his face as he looked at her, I had a feeling he was feeling the same way.

Slightly unnerved, I pulled away from them both.

"Let's get cleaned up," I said, getting to my feet, only a

little unsteady. I needed a minute to compose myself—and Sassy needed to be washed.

A quick dip of a cloth into the basin, I returned to the bed to gently clean Sassy's swollen folds. She murmured, wincing a little and turning on her side. She would be sore tomorrow. Part of me liked knowing she'd still feel us between her thighs. William had risen as well, cleaning himself with another cloth. He handed me a third when I was done with our wife to use on myself.

"Married," William said under his breath, a touch of awe in his tone as he looked down at her. I couldn't stop the smile that curved my lips, and when I looked at him, he had a big, goofy grin on his face.

"Think we need to worry about the man she's running from?" I asked, turning the question over in my mind. We had not needed to talk to know we'd protect a lady in danger, regardless, but we'd want to set a plan in place. We'd need to get his name as well and a description.

Tonight, she'd been safe enough, and likely, she would be tomorrow, but I didn't want to take any chances.

"Don't know." William shrugged, his gaze falling back to her where she was already fast asleep, curled up on her side, away from the candlelight. "We should ask if he was from England or New York."

Farther would be better. Most men would give up, rather than follow a woman this far out west. Sure, there were some who became obsessed, but even those would have to be mightily invested to come this far for a woman. A smart man would cut his losses.

But there were some mighty dumb men out there.

William and I would keep watch. One good thing about living in this area, any strangers arriving, were immediately noticed and remarked upon.

"We'll find out tomorrow," I said, climbing into bed next to Sassy. "If he does show his face, it might be the last thing he ever does."

Our wife sighed in her sleep as William and I bracketed her between us, already protecting her, even though she didn't need it. Nothing and no one would disturb her rest tonight. Snuggling into us, she sighed again, her body relaxing further as if she'd heard the unspoken promise.

Closing my eyes, for the first time in a long time, I dropped off without any trouble.

5

WAKING up with a man in my bed was strange enough, waking up with two of them practically on top of me, I almost giggled once I remembered who they were and why I was in bed with them. I managed to stifle the impulse, not wanting to wake them just yet. I needed a few moments to myself—even if I couldn't move because William had his arm wrapped around my waist, and Clive's legs were draped over mine.

My nipples were still sensitive, and there was an ache between my thighs I hadn't been expecting. Even though it had been a while since I'd plied my former trade, I hadn't thought my body would have changed much.

Then again, no man had ever made me feel the way they had.

The difference between bedding a man who had paid to do so and one who was bedding his wife was greater than I'd imagined.

Making love.

That's what it was called, but we weren't in love, although I could easily imagine myself falling there all too quickly. Already, I unexpectedly felt attached to both of them. The idea I might have brought danger their way did not sit well with me. I'd come for protection but hadn't thought about the safety of those who would be protecting me, not until now.

If either of them was hurt because of me...

I wanted to think Lord Carmichael wouldn't keep following me, but I already knew he'd been looking for me in New York. I hadn't just pricked his pride and stolen from him, I'd injured him. The smell of burning flesh seemed to flood my nose again, and I shuddered, remembering as clear as day the way he'd looked on the floor, moaning while holding his hand to the burn.

"You alright there, sweetheart?" William's low whisper jerked me out of my reverie, the vision and the smell fading as quickly as they'd come. I nodded, turning my head, and meeting his blue eyes, soft and full of concern.

I couldn't have that. Men needed to be happy. To be pleased. My brain was still foggy from sleep, but I remembered that. Reaching out, my fingers quickly found his shaft and wrapped around it. William groaned when I stroked the hard flesh, rubbing my thumb over the sensitive tip.

"I'm fine," I whispered. "I'm just fine."

"Hell, sweetheart, that feels damn good," William whispered, his hand draping over mine.

Good, I was making him feel good. That was what a wife was supposed to do, wasn't it? And I was very good at making men feel good. I propped myself up on my elbow, so I could bend over him, my lips heading for his cock—

Fingers gripped my hair, pulling me back up. I gasped in surprise and the slight pain. William's eyes met mine, a frown forming on his face. He was holding me immobile, thinking hard and staring at me. What had I done wrong? Clive stirred beside us, opening his eyes, but William didn't even glance at him.

"What are you doing, Sassy?" he asked, holding my hair tightly gripped, so I couldn't look away from him.

I wet my lips, my tongue darting out, but he didn't look away from my eyes.

"I-I was just..."

"What was she doing?" Clive asked. Sleep still fogged his voice, but he sat up, clearly coming awake very quickly.

"She was going to use her mouth on me," William said, glancing at Clive.

Now, both of my new husbands were looking at me oddly, chasing the fog from my mind. Panic surged as I realized my sleepy mistake. Whores used their mouths on men. A proper young lady probably shouldn't have even known it was a possibility.

"Where did you learn about that?" Clive asked suspiciously, confirming my thoughts.

"I-I... the girls at the factory," I finally blurted out, hoping with all my heart, they believed the lie. I tripped over my words, trying to find some that wouldn't make them more suspicious. "They said, they said men liked to have their... to be kissed there. Some of them said. Should I... should I not have..." I was stumbling over my words in my panic, very much wishing I had *not* done that, but both William and Clive relaxed at my stammered explanation.

"Well, they weren't wrong," William said, shaking his head almost ruefully, his grip lessening. "Sorry, sweetheart, I shouldn't have reacted that way. I didn't expect you to know about such things, and it took me off guard."

My heart was pounding in my chest, and I bit my lower lip, dropping my head, so they wouldn't see the tears that sprang to my eyes. If I had wanted proof, I couldn't reveal my past to them, I had it. They would surely think differently of me if they knew. Likely treat me differently, too.

Last night, they'd acted as though I was a treasured possession. I did not want to lose that. I did not want to lose them. They clearly thought I was a modest young lady. Would they want to remain married if they knew?

"I'm sorry," I whispered, unsure of what else to say.

"It's fine, sweetheart," William said, stroking my hair. "You just startled me. I'm sorry I overreacted."

Except he hadn't. He'd been right to be shocked. Deep down, I knew that.

This might be harder than I thought.

"We'll teach you how to use your mouth later," Clive said. Unlike William, he wasn't smiling, which made me nervous. A serious expression seemed to be his default, so it might not have meant anything... but I couldn't be sure. "We should get back to the ranch now."

———

Clive

OUR WIFE WAS SOMEWHAT SUBDUED as we packed up our things to head back to the ranch. I kept a close eye on her.

Something about her claim, she'd heard the other factory girls talking about oral pleasure didn't sit right with me. Women gossiped, to be sure, but Sassy was so nervous, even after she'd explained herself. William had believed her story, but I kept watching her, suspicion niggling in the back of my mind.

I didn't know what I was suspicious about, exactly. I just knew that something wasn't quite right. Neither William nor I cared if she had gossiped with other women about sex, but that didn't fit her prim and proper appearance – and I did care if she lied. I didn't like lies.

Some of my doubts from the previous day were seeping back in. After all, what did we really know about her? Only what she told us. And while her story had fit, why did she keep shooting us looks this morning as if she expected us to lash out at her?

While I wanted to trust her, something was amiss. I didn't say anything, though. William was taking everything she said to heart, not a mistrusting bone in his body. He thought I was too cynical, and sometimes, I thought he was right, but something told me our new wife was keeping secrets, even if I couldn't imagine what they would be. Of course, William would likely say it was *me* making her nervous.

If she was lying, I knew of one sure way to make sure she didn't do so again, but I wasn't going to spank her without knowing for sure, no matter how my hand tingled, like a physical portent of things to come.

Getting her seated on the wagon bench between us, I picked up the reins and flicked them to get the horses moving. I let her look her fill of the town, but once we were on the road, I started in with the questions I probably should have asked before we got her in front of the altar.

"So, Sassy. Tell us about this man you're running from."

Out of the corner of my eye, I saw her shoulders tense. I couldn't see her expression because she'd insisted on putting on that ridiculous bonnet again before we'd even left the hotel. It made her feel safer, but it also completely hid her face. Still, if I'd been watching her face, I would have never noticed her shoulders.

William glared at me over her head, but not from my line of questioning. He wanted to know too, just thought I was too blunt.

"Yes, sweetheart, tell us about him," he said more gently, picking up one of her hands to console her. For the first time ever, I was jealous he wasn't holding the reins. Even if I was intent on questioning our new wife, that didn't stop me from wanting to touch her.

"Is he from New York?"

"No, England," she said, her voice soft and throaty. The bonnet twitched as though she'd shaken her head. "He's a lord there. Lord Carmichael. But I know he was looking for me in New York."

The fear was back in her voice and no wonder. A man who was willing to chase her across the ocean was certainly obsessed.

"Do you think knowing you're already married would deter him?" William asked.

Her shoulders hunched in. "I-I don't know... I worry I've brought danger to you."

Despite myself, I was touched. William and I exchanged another look over her head, both of us bemused by her concern.

"That's what we offered, sweetheart. Protection," I drawled. I had full confidence in our ability to protect ourselves *and* her. This Lord Carmichael might think himself powerful, and maybe in England he was, but here in the west, he would find nothing but a bullet between his teeth if he tried to come after our wife.

"That's why I answered your ad," she admitted. "But now that I'm here, I keep thinking how wrong it was to drag someone else into my troubles."

"*Our* troubles," William said, squeezing her hand while I was still groping for the proper words to reassure her. William was good at that. I was better at threats. "You're our wife now, which makes your troubles our troubles. And make no mistake, missy, that's how we want it."

"That's right," I said and meant it. I might want to dig out whatever secrets she was hiding from us, but nothing would change my determination to protect her. I meant that for any woman, but even more so for her. She was our wife. If someone threatened her, he was going to regret it.

———

WILLIAM

WHEN WE REACHED THE RANCH, I helped Sassy down from the wagon while Clive went to unhitch and stable the horses. She pulled off her bonnet, finally, looking up at the house with wide eyes. My cock stirred, and I scooped her up in my arms, wanting to feel her body against mine, even though I didn't plan on making love to her again until tonight.

"William!" she squeaked, flinging her arms around my neck. "What are you doing?"

"Carrying my bride across the threshold," I said with a grin, heading toward the front door.

Sassy glanced over my shoulder, a little furrow of concern appearing on her brow. "What about Clive?"

"He'll get his turn later." If he'd wanted to be the first to carry her into the house, he shouldn't have insisted on being the one to stable the horses. I knew he'd take his time, currying and checking them over before letting them loose in the pasture. I could have done the same, but Clive felt better when he did it.

It wasn't my fault that meant he was missing out on carrying Sassy into the house. Either he'd learn to give up some of his control and let me do more, or he'd miss out on things with Sassy. I was happy to have something to distract me from Clive's lack of trust in my abilities.

I stomped up the stairs to the porch, angling my body, so I could shoulder open the door without loosening my hold on her. She looked around curiously at the main room, which boasted a simple table and chairs, a fire-place and oven, and several shelves on the far wall. In front of the fireplace were two larger chairs where Clive and I sat at the end of the day and chatted about the ranch.

"The house is beautiful," she said with all evidence of sincerity. I couldn't help but raise my eyebrows. It was a decent house but simple. Clive and I didn't have much interest in decorating. Seeing my expression, she shrugged, a little smile curving her lips. "It's clean. Bigger than I'm used to. I never had more than a room, even before my father died."

Her lips clamped shut after the admission, as though she didn't want to say anything else. Did she think I would judge her for being poor?

"It's the nicest house I've ever lived in," I told her, setting her down on her feet. "But then, I didn't have a home at all for a while before I met Clive." Sassy blinked up at me with surprise and concern. Grinning, I ducked down to steal a kiss. I meant it to be a quick one, but once my lips touched hers, my body went up in flames, and I found myself pulling her soft body against mine.

She moaned, her lips parting, and my tongue delved into her mouth. My hands slid over her curves, down to her bottom, pulling her more tightly against me as my cock swelled. I wanted to be inside her again... but there were things to do, and she needed to be shown around the house.

The sound of the door swinging open made me jump, jerking my head up. Clive was standing there, looking at us and shaking his head.

"I leave you alone for five minutes..." he said with a sigh. "Did you show her any of the house?"

Indignation rose, but he wasn't wrong, and my ire mixed with shame that was all too familiar when it came to disappointing Clive. I glared back at him, my jaw clenching. Dressing me down in front of Sassy was a step too far. I was always the one compromising for him because I was the easygoing one, but that didn't mean I was going to let him boss me around when it came to how to handle our wife.

"I was hoping you could show me together," Sassy said, her hand on my chest as she smiled up at Clive. His expression softened, and something inside me eased. She was already acting as a peacemaker between me and Clive, keeping turmoil out of her household.

"Sorry," Clive said, to my surprise. He hardly ever apologized for anything. "I should have thought of that. We can show you around together."

Sassy smiled at him, then at me, a tinge of worry still in her eyes.

"Together," I said, nodding. If Clive and I had it out, it wouldn't be in front of her. Our Sassy wouldn't like us fighting, that was clear. If she could keep Clive more humble than usual, that would help my state of mind considerably.

Placing that ad for a bride had been the best decision I'd ever made. I wouldn't rub it in Clive's nose, though. Not yet.

6

NERVOUSLY WATCHING THE MEN—MY husbands—shovel dinner into their mouths, I felt a small burst of pride. I was no great cook and unused to their kitchen, but I still managed to put together a presentable meal. It felt both odd and very nice to be settled into their home.

Our home.

It would take a while for me to start thinking of it that way.

The men had shown me around, although there hadn't been much more to see than the main room and two bedrooms. William said they'd be turning his old room into a nursery, and we'd be sharing what used to be Clive's room from now on. Outside was a vegetable garden, the outhouse, with a laundry line a little ways away. Tomorrow, I would be able to explore more. Today, we had shared a quick, cold midday meal, then they'd gone off to meet their hands and finish their chores around the ranch, while I unpacked my meager belongings and got to work on familiarizing myself with the kitchen and making dinner.

Now, the sun had gone down, evening was fast approaching, and I was unsettled. After my mistake this morning, I was no longer very confident, although I'd had the afternoon to myself to think about what I should and should not do.

It was going to be difficult, though. My instincts were to try to please them as best I could, but how to do that without revealing I knew more than I should? What should a young woman entering into marriage know? I wished there was another woman who I could talk to, find out what she knew... I hadn't expected to be the only wife, even when I'd seen both men waiting for me at the train station. I thought I'd only be marrying one of them.

But which husband would I be willing to give up having another wife to talk to? William, with his gentle hands, immediate trust, and open emotions, or Clive, with his rough caresses, suspicious looks, and grumpy demeanor?

I looked at them, both men sighing happily as they sat back in their chairs, their plates cleared of all food.

Neither.

I wouldn't want to give up either; I wanted both, felt

attached to both of them. How that had happened so quickly, I did not know.

As if they felt me contemplating them, they lifted their gazes, eyes hot with interest, and my cheeks flushed. They made me feel so... so *much*. I did not even have the word to describe the emotion fluttering through my chest. I also didn't know what to say when they were looking at me as though they wanted to eat me up the way they just had their dinner.

"I, uh... did you enjoy your dinner?" I asked lamely, feeling more than a little foolish. I truly wanted to know, though, which was why the question had popped into my mind.

"Very much," William said, smiling widely. "That was delicious."

Clive nodded in agreement, his expression more sober, but I'd noticed he did not smile much, regardless. I smiled back at both of them, basking in the praise.

"Tomorrow, I'll have dessert," I promised. I'd seen flour, sugar, eggs, and apples in the pantry. It had been years since I'd made a pie, but I thought I still remembered how.

"I think we can still have dessert tonight," William said, his grin widening, heat flaring in his eyes. He pushed his chair back, holding out his hand to me. Confusion flared as I placed my fingers in his. I hadn't seen anything, and I certainly hadn't made anything suitable dessert.

"He's talking about you, Sassy." Clive chuckled, taking

my other hand, standing as well. "You're going to be our dessert."

Me?

I didn't have time to respond before William was tugging me into his arms. This kiss was not as gentle as his previous ones. It was eager and possessive, demanding a response. Clive moved in behind me, pressing a hot kiss to the back of my neck, just under where my hair was wound into a bun on the back of my head.

Heat and need sizzled through me, my senses tingling to life as I was surrounded by their hard bodies.

Oh... I'm the dessert.

Now I understood.

———

Clive

AFTER A LONG DAY on the ranch, coming home to a well-made dinner and a beautiful wife was even more satis-fying than I could have imagined. Now, with Sassy caught between us and my cock already aching to be inside of her, I knew tonight was going to be one to remember—our first night on the ranch with our wife.

My cock ground against the soft curves of her bottom as I held her in place for William, dropping my own kisses along the back of her neck, the curve of her ear, teasing her while he claimed her lips. Watching them together provoked both envy and arousal—not jealousy. No, I liked to watch them kiss… but I also wanted to be part of it.

When William lifted his head, he smiled down at her before turning her my way, so I could have my turn. Instead, I scooped her up in my arms like a bride. Surprised, William stepped back.

"Since William got to carry you over the threshold of our house, I think it's my turn to carry you over the threshold to our bedroom," I said, swinging her around and leading the way.

"I've already been in there today," she pointed out, wrapping her arms around my neck. The feel of her slim fingers against my throat sent a shiver through me.

"That didn't count," I said, shaking my head. "Now, we're going to properly christen the room." Behind me, William chuckled. I carried Sassy like she was the Queen of England, gently letting her feet drop to the floor and holding her against me as she slid down.

That's where I took my kiss from her, pillaging her mouth with all the hot need running through me. Sassy whimpered against my lips, pressing against me, much bolder than she had been the night before. Male satisfaction surged.

She wanted me.

Us.

Wanted *this.*

We'd made her feel good the night before, and now

she wanted more—exactly the way we'd hoped she would.

Sassy was a sensual woman despite her buttoned-up dress. She had been trying to hide her light—no wonder, with a man she didn't want chasing after her—but William and I wanted to see that light. She needn't show it to anyone else. We would make her glow for us and us alone.

Caressing and kissing her, we passed her back and forth, taking turns holding and kissing her breathless while the other undressed her. Each piece of clothing that fell to the floor left her a little more naked, making my cock throb harder until we finally had her completely nude between us.

"So beautiful," William murmured, spinning her back to me again, his eyes wandering over her form and appreciating the sight of both her front and her back—especially her back. Eventually, we would have her between us, taking her at the same time, but that would have to wait. She wasn't ready to know about that yet.

Besides, we had other things to teach her tonight.

"Yes, she is," I agreed, pulling her to me. She tilted her head back, ready for my kiss. Kissing her deeply and thoroughly, making her squirm against my cock gave William the chance to get undressed.

We'd flipped a coin earlier today to see who would have her mouth and who would have her pussy tonight. It had felt a bit crass, but the reason was sound—we didn't want her to be too sore after last night, so we would take turns the next few nights until she was more used to our nightly attentions.

———

SASSY

WHEN CLIVE TURNED me around to face William, he was already naked, sitting on the bed, his hand wrapped around his cock, slowly fisting himself while he watched us kiss. His eyes glinting with appreciation, he smiled at me, a hot, lazy smile that turned my already roiling insides over.

"Come here, beautiful," he said, swinging his legs onto the bed and leaning back against the headboard. He held out his free hand. "You wanted to try using your mouth this morning, well here's your chance."

I took a small step toward him, my mind racing. I was *very* good at using my mouth, but I shouldn't be so good, right? I tried to think back to my early days at Mrs. Burk's house. This had always been a chore, but one I had become accomplished at.

Faced with a man who I actually *wanted* to pleasure for myself rather than to earn my keep, it was hard knowing I could not show him the full extent of my skill. I remembered my initial distaste, how my jaw ached. Gagging. I doubted William would slap me if I accidentally used my teeth, but I didn't want to, but wouldn't a woman who didn't know what she was doing?

How ironic that I was standing in front of a man I desired, my mouth actually watering, wanting to give him all the pleasure I could... but doing so would likely make him turn from me in disgust.

"Feeling shy now?" Clive asked, chuckling in my ear. His hand on my back moved me forward, gently but firmly. "Go on, sweetheart. William will guide you."

He gave my bottom a little smack, and I jumped in surprise. It stung but didn't truly hurt. Still, I shot him a dark look over my shoulder as I rubbed the spot where he'd swatted me. Clive just chuckled.

"Get a move on, sweetheart." Clearly, my glare didn't intimidate him at all.

Strangely, the little interaction had helped clear my head, easing my nerves. William was going to guide me. I would just follow his lead and do what he told me. It helped that Clive seemed to think my hesitation was because I didn't know what I was doing, not because I knew too much.

Hesitation was good.

I slowly moved to the bed, taking William's hand, and letting him pull me up to where I knelt between his legs. He let go of his cock, bringing my hand to the hot, hard shaft, replacing his grip, and wrapped my fingers around him. He kept his hand over mine and moved it, so I was stroking his cock under his direction while he stared at me with erotic intensity.

I watched our hands move, fascinated by how enjoyable I found the procedure and how gentle he was, showing me what he liked. The desire to please him surged. I wanted to give him everything.

His free hand slid into my hair, tugging me closer.

"Lean over and lick me above our hands," he said, using his hand to guide my head down. I hesitated again, not because I wanted to—I was eager to have him in my mouth, which was a shock in and of itself—but I worried what he would think if I didn't. His hand tugged gently, and I followed his instruction.

I delicately licked, a tiny lick as if I was trying it out. William shuddered at the small touch, and a surprising feeling of power surged. I had never felt powerful in this position before. Men had used my mouth, and I was good at pleasing them with it, but this felt different.

"Good girl. Use your tongue over the whole head," William directed, his voice raspy.

Out of the corner of my eye, I could see Clive watching us as he undressed, and feeling his eyes on us, heated my body even more. I felt wanton but beautiful under their lustful gazes.

Cherished.

I felt cherished—just as they'd promised.

My heart clenched, emotions swelling.

William groaned, and I realized I was licking him with abandon, my tongue swirling around the bulbous head of his cock and flicking over the sensitive slit, my fingers moving up and down his shaft of their own accord.

Too good. Too experienced.

I jerked back.

"No, no, don't stop, that was perfect," William said, opening his eyes and pulling my head back down with the hand still entangled in my hair. "The groan was a good thing."

I bit my lower lip, peeking up at him, grateful he was willing to find reasons for my reactions that suited his image of me.

"If you're sure..."

"Oh, believe me, sweetheart," William chuckled, "I'm sure." He pushed my hand down to the base of his shaft. "Keep using your tongue, and when you're ready, take my cock in your mouth and suck. You can hold the base with your hand to keep me from going too deep."

Of course. Do not swallow the whole thing. I certainly hadn't been able to do so when I'd first learned how to pleasure a man with my mouth.

Let William guide you

That was exactly what I was going to do.

Clive moved toward us.

"She'll look so pretty with your cock in her mouth," he said gruffly but sincerely. He didn't seem completely comfortable with the dirty words, unlike William, but he was trying.

I smiled shyly, turning my head slightly, so he could watch as I licked the crown of William's cock, moving my lips over its surface. Heat flared in Clive's eyes. He began stroking his own cock while he watched, moving even closer, so he could run his hand down my back and over my bottom.

I gasped when I felt his finger slide between my cheeks, finding the crinkled star there. He rubbed gently, but only for a moment before his fingers moved again, seeking and finding the wet, swollen folds of my pussy. His fingers slipped into the folds, and I moaned, opening my lips and bending my head over William's cock, stifling the sound.

William groaned with me, his hand tightening in my hair. I sucked hard, turning my growing need into his pleasure. Clive's fingers explored my slippery folds, probing and teasing, making me whimper around William's cock. My lips touched my fingers, and I realized I was forgetting myself.

I had to remember to pretend I was new to this.

But then Clive climbed onto the bed behind me, lifting my hips, so I was on my knees before him, my head bent over William's lap, and all thoughts flew out of my head.

 illiam

SASSY'S MOUTH wrapped around my cock was the second-best thing I'd ever felt, right after her pussy on my cock. She'd been a little hesitant at first, but once Clive started touching her, she'd stopped thinking about what she was doing, and I was reaping the benefits.

It was as though she was taking out her own arousal on me, the sensations Clive was creating in her transferred directly to me as she licked and sucked, her mouth sliding further down my shaft, the more Clive's fingers teased her. Her tongue fluttered against the underside of my cock, and I groaned, winding her long, dark hair about my fist, using it to help anchor myself while keeping it out of her way.

I liked being able to see her face while she bobbed her head up and down on my cock—the way her eyelashes fluttered, the flush growing on her cheeks, and the way her plush lips stretched around my glistening shaft. The vibrations of her hums and moans went straight through me and up my spine, adding to my pleasure.

She was a damn natural at this.

Clive climbed onto the bed behind her, his gaze fixed on her upturned ass. I held her hair a little more tightly, reaching beneath her with my other hand to fondle one of her plump breasts. She mewled, the suction on my cock increasing, and I pinched her nipple in response. My hips thrust, pushing me a little deeper into her mouth, and I felt her gag slightly. Her hand tightened around the base of my cock.

"Yes, just like that," I said, panting for breath. Squeezing her breast, I did my best to lie still as Clive lined himself up with her pussy from behind.

I could tell the moment he began to slide into her, because she sucked even harder, her fingers moving with her lips, her whimpering moans muffled by my cock. Tightly gripping the reins of my growing need, I laid back against the pillows, determined to keep my climax at bay, so I could enjoy this for as long as possible.

Watching Clive grip Sassy's hips and thrust forward, pure pleasure filling his expression while Sassy cried out around my cock, I couldn't be sure it was going to be very long at all.

Sassy

ONE MAN in front of me, one man behind me, both of them filling me at the same time... this was something with which I had no experience. Just like I had no experience with the rush of emotion that flowed through me as I was impaled by both of my husbands.

My desire to please had always been part of knowing my income depended on it, not from anything within myself. But I wanted to please _them_, with no ulterior motive—nothing but a deep desire to see their gratification and know I was its cause.

William's hand on my breast caressed, while Clive's fingers dug into my hips, holding me in place. He thrust, and I cried out, rocking forward, William's cock sliding deeper between my lips. My throat worked, swallowing him as my fingers fell away.

I was lost in a haze of lust and pleasure, my hands braced on either side of William's hips as I was pushed back and forth between them. Clive kept a tight grip on my hips, thrusting harder and faster, and I tightened around him as my pleasure grew. I could no longer focus on what I was doing to Will, but it hardly mattered.

I could tell from his hard grip on my hair, the way his hips thrust upward, using my mouth, he was enjoying himself. I breathed in as much as I could between strokes, the lack of air beginning to make me dizzy, which somehow added to my growing ecstasy.

I shuddered between them, letting myself revel in the sensations running through my body. Just like the night before, I could feel something inside of me coiling and winding tighter and tighter. The needy ache between my thighs was approaching a pinnacle, and my body yearned for it, reached for it. I craved the bliss I'd found with them the night before.

"Oh, hell..." Clive's fingers tightened on my hips, and his thrusts slowed as if he was trying to hold back and take his time. I wriggled in protest. I wanted more— harder, faster. I needed it.

Instead, his hand moved, sliding over my bottom, and I tensed when I felt him touch the little hole between my cheeks again. Did he mean to have me there? Fear flickered through my passion. I had never had a man take me there without pain, but... if there were any men who were worth enduring it for, it was Clive and William.

His hand disappeared for a moment, then returned, his slicked thumb circling over the rim of my tight entrance, surprising me with a sizzle of pleasure. Then he pressed, and I whined around William's cock, wriggling and squirming between them. My muscles clenched down, making it more difficult for him to gain entrance, but the slow pressure did the trick.

Surprisingly, it didn't hurt.

There was a slight burn as his thumb entered, stretching me open, but little more than a sting. In fact, it almost felt good. His thumb pressed deeper as his cock thrust slowly in and out of me, and I squirmed and clenched around him. I felt so very full, almost too full, but it made me hotter... wetter...

These men were completely upending everything I'd learned at Mrs. Burk's.

"Good girl," William crooned, clearly aware of what Clive was doing. "Doesn't that feel good?"

I moaned around his cock in answer, unable to do anything else. With his thumb buried between my cheeks, Clive was moving again, thrusting harder and faster, while William's cock thrust between my lips.

"We're both going to have you one day," William whispered, his words weaving a perverse spell. "One of us beneath you in your sweet pussy, one of us behind you, taking your ass, making you so full and hot, you'll barely be able to breathe."

I could barely breathe now, my eyes glazing over as the image he described filled my head. It was utterly erotically wicked. Even my fear of the pain I remembered from other men buggering me didn't put me off. It wove through my arousal, William and Clive's hands and bodies driving away the memories, giving me new fantasies in their place.

"I think she likes that idea," Clive said with a chuckle, his thumb moving inside me, rubbing his cock through the thin lining between my holes.

I should have been afraid, but I wasn't. I trusted them not to hurt me.

What they were doing to me felt good. Clive's thumb and cock felt good. Perhaps having one of them in each channel would feel good as well. Nestled between them, the way William described, certainly would.

Leaning forward, Clive rode me in earnest, and I cried out with growing rapture, filling my mouth with William's cock as my passion soared. I was so full of them, in every orifice possible, my ecstasy could no longer be contained.

Quivering, shuddering, I lost myself in the hot bliss of climax, buffeted between them as wave after wave of rapture washed over me. I could feel Clive's cock thrusting deep and pulsing inside me only moments before William's grip tightened on my hair, and he emptied himself down my throat.

I was so wonderfully, obscenely full of them... my husbands. Euphoria moved through me, and I gave myself to it completely.

Clive

WE'D WORN our Sassy out again, although she did manage to give both of us a sleepy goodnight kiss before she fell asleep.

Although William and I were tired, neither of us was ready to lie down yet, and there were dishes to be done. Normally, we'd let Sassy tend to them, but as we were the ones who had worn her out... Besides, dishes were no hardship.

"I think we're going to need to talk to Rhys about getting her a plug as soon as possible," William said, sounding amused as he shut the bedroom door behind him. Like me, he hadn't bothered putting on a shirt, although we'd both pulled our pants on.

Yes, we were. I chuckled. Rhys made handcrafted plugs to help train a woman's bottom to be ready for her husbands. Sassy had frozen up when I'd first touched her tiny hole, but she'd relaxed once she realized I wasn't hurting her. I was a bit surprised, though. I'd expected more of a fight since it was such a private area.

"Definitely," I agreed, collecting the dishes from the table while William got the water and soap. "Although you seemed to enjoy her mouth just fine."

"That I did." William grinned. "She's a natural, I tell you. Sweet as honey and twice as fine. We're lucky as hell."

That we were, although something niggled at me about what he said. I couldn't put my finger on what was bothering me, so I pushed it away for now.

"We should talk to Sheriff Baker and Hank, too," I said. "Just in case Lord Carmichael comes looking for her." My lip curled up in a sneer at his name.

William nodded, his expression turning dark and

fierce with an expression I'd never seen before. Then again, we'd never had a wife to protect. We had a ranch to protect, but that was hardly the same thing, and there was no human threat to our land or cattle.

"If he does, he can turn right around, or he won't be leaving at all," William said, his voice hard and uncompromising. He almost sounded like me. After a pause, he spoke again, his voice softer. "I'd rather he not show at all, though. I think it would upset Sassy."

"That would be for the best." Normally, I'd be one for facing a threat and dealing with it, but in this, Sassy's feelings would come first. "Do you think we should ask Ford if he knows anything about Carmichael?"

Like us, Ford was fairly new to town and a former lord himself, a marquess or something like that. Titles didn't mean anything in Bridgewater, so I hadn't paid much attention to the details. He was a good man, happily married in the Bridgewater way, sharing a bride with one of the soldiers who had traveled with him.

William nodded slowly. "More information can't hurt. We should probably question Sassy once she's more comfortable."

Truthfully, I wanted to question her immediately, but her reluctance to talk about her past was fairly clear. Hopefully, William was right, and she'd eventually answer our questions without hesitation. She was so giving with her body, but she held back with her thoughts.

I wanted both and knew William felt the same.

Lost in our own thoughts, we got the kitchen cleaned up and returned to the bedroom, stripping before climbing in on either side of her. Her soft, warm skin brushed against mine, and my cock immediately twitched with interest, but I ignored it. Securing our wife between us, William and I quickly fell asleep.

8

OVER THE NEXT couple of days, I discovered life on a ranch was both easier and harder than I'd imagined.

The mornings came quickly, far more quickly than I was used to, even when I'd been working in the factory. I adjusted, though, eagerly plunging into my new life and trying to push away the nagging worries that had followed me out west. It was easier to forget Lord Carmichael and the possible danger when my husbands were at home, but they couldn't be there all day.

It shocked me how quickly I grew to crave their presence. I didn't care how dirty and sweaty they were when they reached the front door, I would fly into their arms for a greeting. Clive had been startled at first, although William met me with a wide grin.

At night, they told me stories about their day on the ranch, answered my questions, and took me out to the barn to meet the horses and barn cats before we retired to the bedroom. They took turns in my mouth and pussy, sometimes using their mouths and fingers on me first, and always, *always*, bringing me to my pleasure before they took theirs.

Both of them also spent a good deal of time stretching out my bottom, using their fingers, to the point where my fear had receded, and I was beginning to crave having them fill me completely. They had already shown me how much pleasure they could give me that I had never experienced before... maybe this would be the same.

Even if it wasn't, I truly wanted to please them so much, I would endure whatever they wished in order to satisfy them.

One afternoon, William came riding back to the house, startling me where I was hanging our laundry to dry. Quickly, I strung up the last of the wash, so I could be done by the time he arrived. He didn't seem to be in a particular hurry to reach me, but concern rose up, none-theless. Frowning, I came out from behind the line, having pinned the last sheet in place.

"Is everything well?" I asked as he rode up. "Is Clive alright?"

The smile that flashed across William's face was surprisingly wicked, and I blinked in surprise. I'd been sure that something was wrong. Had he come back to the house just to make love to me?

"Clive is fine," William said reassuringly. He leaned to the side, reaching for me with his hand. "Come here, I'll take you back to the house. I have something for you."

My interest piqued, I took his hand and let him pull me onto his lap on the horse, then gave me a thorough kiss that sent tingles through me.

I desperately wanted to learn how to ride, but the men hadn't had time to teach me yet. Sitting on William or Clive's lap while they rode was the best they'd been able to do so far, and I loved every moment of it. To be truthful, sitting on their laps was certainly no hardship. I loved the feel of them holding onto me tightly, knowing they would keep me safe and secure.

Even though the ride lasted less than a minute, since the laundry line was just behind the house, my body was already humming from William's touch. My nipples hardened, and my pussy creamed in anticipation.

———

WILLIAM

WHY HAD I thought it was a good idea to put my wife on my lap when I knew I wasn't going to have time to indulge her?

The moment her soft curves hit my thighs, my cock

went from interested to full mast. Having her ride with me was exquisite torture. She was a soft weight, her bottom rubbing against my cock, my arm banded about her middle just under her breasts, and the sweet, floral scent of her skin filling my nose. I was going to miss this once we taught her how to ride.

Maybe we'd still occasionally take rides like this for old time's sake.

Letting her slip off Blaze, I followed her down, hitching the horse to the front porch. Sassy's eyebrows rose.

"I take it this won't be a long visit?" she asked, her lips curving upwards. She cocked her head at me, clearly curious.

"Like I said, just something to give you." My eyes sparkled with mischief as I pulled the box Rhys had brought to us out of my saddlebag. He'd swung by while we were out in the fields. Sassy reached for it, but I waved her hands away. "No, no, let's go in the house, so I can give it to you properly."

Confused but curious, she preceded me into the house before spinning around and putting her hands on her hips.

"Can you give it to me now?"

Instead of answering, I pointed to the table.

"Go bend over the table, sweetheart, and close your eyes."

"I am becoming very suspicious of this present,

husband." She sighed, shaking her head in mock exasperation.

Chuckling, I followed along behind her. "Trust me, wife."

Quietly, so quietly I almost didn't hear her, she murmured, "I do."

I practically glowed at her admission, my chest tightening with emotion. She trusted me completely and without reservation. Not even Clive trusted me that way —he needed to be in control too much—but our wife did. I didn't have the words to tell her how much that meant to me, but I would find a way to show her.

For now, I needed to give her the present.

She bent over the table, exactly as I'd asked. I flipped her skirts up, baring her from the waist down, and Sassy squeaked, wriggling her beautiful bottom. Her pussy was already plump and glossy with her arousal, and my cock jerked. It felt almost wrong to have her in this position and *not* plunge into her, but I needed to get back to Clive in the fields.

I had won the coin toss to deliver Rhys' gift since both of us wanted to start her bottom training as quickly as possible, but Clive wouldn't take it well if I dallied, and I wouldn't blame him. While we might take turns having Sassy to ourselves at some point, that would need to be agreed upon beforehand.

Sassy looked over her shoulder, craning her neck to see what I was doing as I pulled one of the polished wooden plugs out of the box. We'd ordered three from Rhys, in growing sizes, and I'd picked up the smallest.

"What is that?" she asked, pushing herself up with her hands to see better.

I swatted her bottom. "Back down on the table, sweetheart."

With a disappointed *humph*, she lowered back down while I oiled the wood, making it nice and slick and even shinier than it already was.

"These are going to help get your bottom ready for Clive and me," I told her, making sure its surface was nice and slick. "It's called a plug. Today you're just going to wear it for the afternoon while you get used to it."

She gasped when I pressed the tip to her bottom and began to push in, already squirming at the sensation. My cock throbbed in protest of its confinement. Ignoring the need pulsing through me, I concentrated on gently opening up Sassy's bottom, moving the plug back and forth with little motions, pushing it deeper.

———

Sassy

Oh, my...

My fingers gripped the edge of the table, and I gasped at the sensation of being stretched open. I had become accustomed to a finger or two when Clive or

William had his mouth on my pussy, but this was different.

It was harder, thicker, and there was nothing to distract me from the slow burn of penetration as William worked the plug back and forth inside me.

My bottom clenched, trying to keep out the invader.

"Just relax, sweetheart," William said, and I moaned when he touched my clit, rubbing in slow, firm circles that made my toes curl. "It will be easier if you relax."

Easy for him to say. He wasn't the one having something pushed up his bottom. It *didn't* hurt, other than a slight burn. I trusted him, so I tried to relax. His fingers circling my clit added to the growing pleasure, which far outweighed the discomfort from the plug.

It nosed deeper, and I yelped at the tiny sting as it suddenly popped through the tight ring of my entrance. Now snugly fitted inside of me, I could feel it pressing on my insides, filling me even more than their fingers and with far more resistance.

"Good girl," William said, giving my pussy a final pat before pulling down my skirts.

Indignant, I shot straight up to a standing position, which made my bottom clench around the plug. I gasped at the sensation, unable to focus for a moment.

"Whoa there!" William grabbed my elbow, keeping me from swaying too much. "Alright, sweetheart?"

Was I alright? Oh... no. No, I was not.

"No!" I glared at him. "I'm all heated up, but I didn't... you didn't..." I blushed hard. Not because dirty words intimidated me, but because asking for what I wanted felt so unfamiliar.

"Well, now you know how I feel," he said with a wink. I scowled, but he pulled me into his arms, kissing the frown from my lips before pulling away. "Don't take that out unless you need to use the outhouse. Clive and I will be back at our regular time." He sauntered out of the house, hard cock pressed against the front of his pants as if he hadn't a care in the world.

My scowl returned, and I looked down my front. My body was so ready, so primed, maybe I didn't need my husbands for what I wanted... The front door opened, and I jumped in surprise, heart in my throat, but it was just William again. He pointed a stern finger at me.

"No touching yourself while we're away, Sassy." His expression was so forthright, I knew he was serious. "Clive and I will take care of your pleasure tonight." Then he was gone again.

Scowling, I kicked the table leg in frustration, which made the plug jostle. My body pulsed, and I whimpered. Taking a deep breath, I decided I needed to find a chore to distract myself. What had I been going to do next?

Oh, yes, water the garden with the water from the wash.

Every step was erotic torture. The plug moved, making me think about William and Clive and what they wanted to do to me, which aroused me even further. My pussy was slick and swollen, the lips rubbing together and heating my insides. I wanted to touch myself so badly...

But I didn't want to disappoint my husbands.

The afternoon passed far more quickly than I could have countenanced, likely due to my distracted state. I put together a dinner of beans and ham, letting it simmer in its pot while my fresh-baked bread was wrapped in a cloth on the table. Easy to eat and, more importantly to my mind, the beans and ham wouldn't suffer from extra simmering.

As soon as I heard the clump of boots making their way to the front door, I hurried to greet my husbands. My body was aching, and I was going to explode if I didn't get some satisfaction soon. Before they even had a chance to open the door, I flung it open and threw myself at them.

Clive's eyes went wide with surprise, but he caught me easily.

"Sassy? What—"

I cut him off, pulling his head down and kissing him with all the desperation and erotic frustration the afternoon had ignited inside me.

live

WILLIAM HAD TOLD me he'd left our wife wanting, but I don't think either of us could have expected how desperate she'd become, waiting for us.

She hit me with the force of a runaway horse, body careening into mine, arms wrapping around my neck and pulling me down to her as her lips came up to me. Sassy was a sensual woman, eager to please William and me in the bedroom, but she'd never been like *this*.

Her kiss was demanding but pleading, her hands already moving down my collar to the buttons down the front of my shirt as if she couldn't get me undressed fast enough. My cock had turned rock-hard so fast, I was dizzy. I kissed her back, responding to her need, my hands groping her bottom and pulling at her skirt.

Behind me, William chuckled.

"Don't you think you should get her in the house before you two get naked, Clive?" William chided, not quite scolding—a tone I recognized as one I often used on him.

I felt my cheeks turn red as I lifted my lips from hers. I had actually forgotten where we were standing. Sassy affected me so strongly, I hadn't been thinking... hadn't cared.

"Of course," I said gruffly, sweeping her up in my arms to carry her into the house, pretending I hadn't completely lost my head over her kiss. Sassy squirmed in my arms, panting, her cheeks flushed with arousal.

"Wait, where's my hello kiss?" William complained, following us in.

Sassy glared at him over my shoulder. "*You*?! You put that thing in me, then left me, here without letting me climax!"

Ah, so our girl could hold a grudge. Good to know. I chuckled, no longer feeling so envious about William winning our coin toss earlier. I'd been tormented all afternoon while I was working, wishing I'd been able to watch as her bottom took the plug for the first time and see her reactions firsthand. Still, I had some sympathy for William since it could have just as easily been me in his position. I patted Sassy's bottom before setting her down.

"And you better not have brought yourself off while you were waiting for us."

Turning her glare on me, she was squirming and jittery, panting for breath. Her nipples were hard nubs, pressing against the front of her dress, begging to be touched, sucked. My mouth watered in anticipation.

"Does it look like I gave myself any satisfaction?" she snapped.

William and I exchanged a look. She was bordering on being disrespectful. My palm started to itch, but she hadn't quite crossed the line to where we'd spank her. Yet.

"She's not used to this," William said, understanding where my thoughts were leading. He frowned at Sassy. "I —we—understand you're frustrated, but that doesn't excuse rudeness."

"As if you wouldn't be rude in my circumstances?" She looked aghast.

"We've been in your circumstances all day," I said, reaching out to take her hand and place her palm over the bulge at the front of my pants. I groaned as her fingers curved around it, giving me the first sense of relief I'd had all afternoon. "I've been hard as a rock, thinking about you back here, plugged, wet, and waiting for us."

Sassy stared up at me, eyes wide and lips slightly parted. Her little pink tongue flicked out, wetting her lips, trying to figure out whether she wanted to snap again, or if she wanted her orgasm.

"Me, too." William walked up to her other side and took her hand, placing it over his own contained erection.

———

Sassy

I WANTED to yell at William that he could have taken care of that *earlier* for *both* of us... but then that wouldn't have been very fair to Clive, would it? I sighed, closed my eyes, and let myself enjoy the hard bulges under the rough fabric of their pants. At least I hadn't been the only one suffering this afternoon.

What did they say? Misery loves company. But there were far more fun things to do together than be miserable.

My husbands crowded around me, their hands sliding over my body, their lips pressing against either side of my neck, and I whimpered as I clenched around the plug. I was so full, yet so empty. My pussy pulsed with need, and my clit throbbing between my thighs.

Hands plumped my breasts, and someone pulled on my hair, tugging my head back. William's lips pressed against mine while Clive's teeth scraped over the delicate skin of my collarbone. My body was burning up with a need I'd never experienced.

"Please," I begged when William's lips lifted. "Don't tease me anymore. I can't take it." I didn't want to be teased—I wanted to be *taken*. If they teased me anymore, my body felt as if it would shatter into pieces, unable to sustain the level of need wound so tightly inside.

"As you wish," William said, exchanging one of those looks with Clive, where they seemed to read each other's mind.

The next thing I knew, I was lifted onto the table and laid out on my back. William flipped my skirts up, stepped between my legs, and hooked his arms beneath them, lifting and spreading my thighs apart. He did not even remove our clothes, just opened the front of his pants, his cock springing free, so he could slide right into me.

Crying out, my body arched as he filled me with one smooth thrust, his cock shoving in and fighting with the plug for space. Sparks kindled through my body, and my muscles clenched down around him and the plug, making William throw back his head and groan.

Clive took my hand—I hadn't even noticed him coming around to the side of the table—and wrapped it around his cock before he fondled my breasts. I squeezed the thick organ, my arm automatically pumping, although I couldn't focus on what I was doing. Not with William thrusting, hard and fast just like I needed, while Clive squeezed my breasts.

I writhed, the sudden maelstrom of sensations over-whelming me. I had gone from a plug, sitting quietly in my bottom, titillating and arousing me, to being fucked by one husband while the other tormented my breasts. Clive pulled open the top of my dress, giving him better access to pinch and tug on my nipples, and I keened at the hot burst of pleasure.

William groaned, fucking me harder, faster. My pussy slickly contracted around him, and I cried out with exultant abandon as I finally reached my peak. The anticipation throughout the afternoon had primed my body, and I was reaping the benefits.

The climax was even more intense than usual, whether from the long wait or from my muscles spasming around the plug in my bottom, it was impossible to say. I sobbed with ecstasy, tears sliding down the sides of my cheeks as every inch of my body buzzed and hummed from their expert assault.

"Hell... Sassy... you feel so damn good..." William thrust in hard, and I felt him throbbing and filling me with his seed. I slumped beneath him, panting, my own release finally wrung out of me, leaving me breathless and spent. He leaned over me for a long moment with his eyes closed before his cock began to soften inside me.

I already felt wrung out from finally achieving my long-awaited orgasm... but I still had another husband to satisfy.

I gasped when Clive rolled me over onto my stomach, and my stiff, tingling nipples met the cool wood of the table. After all his pinching and tugging, they were more sensitive than usual, and any movement against the hard surface made them prickle pleasurably. I laid my cheek against the table, meeting William's eyes. He gave me a lazy grin.

My skirts, which had fallen over my legs when I rolled, were flipped up, baring my bottom. Fingers gripped my hips, and the head of his cock rubbed against my slick, swollen pussy. I whimpered as little zings of pleasure sizzled through my insides, feeling exquisitely sensitive after William's rough pounding and my own intense orgasm.

Not that I would ask Clive to stop.

He thrust in just as hard and fast as William had, and I cried out, shutting my eyes against William's avid expression as he watched Clive ride me. The new position meant every time Clive slammed home, his body pressed against the base of the plug, making it feel as though both it and his cock were shoving into me at once. My body spasmed around the invaders, the powerful stimulation making my senses shriek.

Clive's fingers gripped my hips tightly, pinning me to the table in a feat of fierce, raw lust, he vented on my all-too-willing body. Even as tears began to slide down my cheeks again, the intensity of the pleasure running through me becoming almost painful, I loved every second of it.

The feeling of him inside me, the slippery wetness of William's cum easing his passage, William's eyes watching us with pleasure, even though he'd already taken his fill...

It was savagely intimate and entirely satisfying.

He buried himself in my pussy, and I cried out as his cock pressed against a spot deep inside. My whole body seized and quaked, muscles clutching his cock and the plug, sending me soaring with rapture and milking him as he came.

Completely limp from pleasure, I sighed with utter repletion.

———

WILLIAM

WATCHING Clive take our wife stirred my cock, even though it had only been mere minutes since I'd had her. If I wasn't so damn hungry for actual food, I might have stepped up for a second, slower turn with our wife, but that could wait for later. My stomach growled in agreement. It had been a long day, although I'd enjoyed the homecoming.

Clive pulled away from Sassy with a satisfied sigh that matched my sentiments. She opened her eyes, but I could tell she wasn't seeing me even though she was looking at me. There was a happy little smile on her face that made my heart pound with something other than lust.

Something sweeter.

Something softer.

Dinner was delicious, as always, and Sassy had baked us cookies for dessert, although she called them 'biscuits' to my and Clive's amusement. I'd have to give her my ma's recipe for real biscuits... I just had to remember where I'd put it. Unlike Sassy, neither Clive nor I had any skill at baking. She seemed to enjoy it, though, and we certainly enjoyed her efforts.

Unfortunately, there was also something we needed to discuss before bed that would put a bit of a damper on things. I cleared my throat.

"Sassy, what can you tell us about Lord Carmichael?"

Our wife froze in her seat, dark eyes opening wide, full of fear.

"Wh-what do you need to know?"

The tremor in her voice was enough to have Clive and me scooting closer to her, protectively offering our reassurance. We each took a hand, bolstering her from either side.

"Clive is going into town tomorrow to speak to the sheriff." I caressed the soft skin of her hand with my thumb, trying to soothe her.

"I meant to go before this, but we had some catching up to do on the ranch after the wedding," Clive said.

We weren't a big operation, and with both of us away from the ranch at the same time, our workers took the brunt of it while we were away, but none of them had complained. They understood and were happy for us, but we hadn't felt comfortable taking any time away until today when I'd come to the house to plug Sassy. Tomorrow, it would be Clive's turn, although he'd be going into town since we'd take care of plugging our wife before we left for the day.

"It's unlikely he'll be able to follow you out here, even if he wanted to," Clive said confidently. "But we won't take any chances with your safety. I want Sheriff Baker to know there might be people asking after you and not to tell them anything. I'll also tell him whatever I can about Carmichael, so he can be on the lookout."

Sassy stared at the table, not meeting our eyes. Clive and I exchanged a worried glance over her head. She had told us about growing up in London, and we knew she hadn't been rich and about her father before his death, but she never brought up the man she'd been running from. Clive still thought there was something she wasn't telling us since most men would give up when a woman ran clear across the world to escape him, but I pointed out he'd already followed her to New York.

Neither of us understood a man who wouldn't heed the word 'no,' but neither of us had ever been a lord, so we couldn't begin to guess at his motivations.

"He has dark hair and eyes and..." She closed her eyes, swallowing hard. "I doubt he'd come for me himself. Not all the way out here when he couldn't be sure he'd find me. I hope." Her breath stuttered. "I *never* want to see him again."

"Easy there," I crooned, sliding my arm around her shoulders, using the same tone of voice I would on a fractious horse. "You won't have to, sweetheart. We'll keep you safe. I promise."

Sassy finally looked up, meeting my gaze, and she smiled.

"I know. You two have made me feel safe for the first time in... well, in a very long time."

"Well, that is what the ad promised," Clive said, amused. I shot him a glare over Sassy's head.

"Can we just go to bed and not talk about him?" Sassy pleaded prettily, looking back and forth between us. "I hate talking about him. Just saying his name taints the room with his presence."

"Fair enough," I said. Clive frowned but didn't gainsay me, which was a bit of a surprise. Sassy had softened him. He wasn't quite as bossy as he used to be. Looking back at our wife, my cock began to harden in anticipation. "Let's go to bed, and your husbands will make sure you forget all about him."

"Oh, will they?" Sassy sassed, raising one eyebrow as I helped her to her feet. Clive smirked.

Yes, we would.

After teasing her with the plug and our fingers, suckling her breasts at the same time until she was begging us to take her, I put her on top of me, facing away, so I could play with the base of the plug. Clive stood over my legs, feeding her his cock while she bounced up and down on mine.

By the end, Sassy fell straight to sleep with a smile on her face, as promised. Our sweet wife. The emotions in my chest swelled.

Cherished and protected. That's what we had promised, and that's what we would give her.

live

THE JAIL WAS empty when I walked in, except for Sheriff Baker. Sitting at his desk reading a newspaper, he looked up sharply when I entered. Seeing my calm demeanor, he relaxed.

"Howdy, Sheriff." I nodded my head in greeting.

"Howdy, Clive," he said, putting down the newspaper with a smile. "What brings you here today?"

"Just need a minute, Sheriff." I took the seat across from him, leaning back wearily. I was more tired since Sassy came into our lives, although I didn't regret it one bit. "It's probably nothing, but my and William's new bride might have a problem that will follow her here, and we just want to make sure she's safe."

"That's right, I'd heard about the wedding," Sheriff Baker said, a grin splitting open his face. "Congratulations. When do we get to meet the lucky lady?"

"We should be at church next week." We'd missed the past Sunday's service, but we usually managed to attend. It was the most regular socializing we did since both William and I were homebodies. The saloon had never much appealed to either of us.

With Sassy at home, we were even more inclined to stay at home for the most part, but we also wanted to show her off and give her a chance to meet the neighbors.

"I'm looking forward to meeting her. So, what kind of trouble is she running from?" He put his arms on his desk, leaning forward, eyes serious.

"A man who wanted her," I said, my lips twisting. "His name is Lord Carmichael. She hasn't said much, but she's scared to death of him. He followed her all the way from England to New York." As I spoke, Sheriff Baker began to frown. Women around here were protected and respected, and I knew he'd seriously take even a slight threat to one. "I doubt he'd even know how or where to find her, but William and I want to make sure we've done everything we can to keep her safe."

Sheriff Baker rubbed his chin. "Your Sassy... what does she look like?"

There was something about the way he asked that made my hackles rise. "Why?"

He gave me a look. "Just tell me, please."

I straightened in the chair, no longer relaxed.

"Not too tall but not too short, she comes to just under my chin when she's standing straight. Long black hair and dark eyes, light tan to her skin, and..." I hesitated but foraged on. I didn't want to sound like I was bragging but also wanted to tell the truth. "She's gorgeous. One of the most beautiful women I've ever seen, although she did her best to hide it on the way here. I can understand why a man would become obsessed with her, although he should have respected her rejection."

William and I certainly had, in our own way, but since that happened after we'd married her, it was hardly the same thing.

The expression on the Sheriff's face had become blank. I couldn't tell what he was thinking, let alone feeling, making me even more worried. A long moment of silence stretched between us as if he couldn't quite figure out what to say to me. I gripped the arms of the chair.

"Say whatever it is you need to say, Sheriff."

"I think someone might already be in the area, looking for her." The Sheriff met my eyes, looking almost sad. My chest tightened with fear, and I had to push down the urge to jump up and rush back to the ranch. I could tell he had more to say. "There are some men who have been asking around. They showed up two days ago, looking for someone who sounds like her, but..."

"But what?" I barked out harshly, demanding an answer. "I don't like this game you're playing."

"No game." He shook his head. "But the story they're

telling is very different. The woman they're looking for was a man's mistress. She stole from him and assaulted him before fleeing, scarring him, and will likely be hanged when she's returned to London for her crimes."

"His mistress?" I asked, my lips and tongue feeling strangely swollen as I repeated his words. My thoughts were galloping away. It would explain... a lot. William and I had talked about what a quick learner she was, how eager, how sensual. Experience would explain that.

"They said she was a whore before that, in a brothel." The Sheriff sounded almost apologetic. "They were looking for her in the saloon at first. No one has seen a woman meeting that description, though, so they've had no luck."

She'd lied.

Lied about everything.

"And she's a thief, too?" I asked. "She assaulted him?"

"*If* it's the same woman," the Sheriff said, looking at me worriedly. "Son, I'm not sure that it is, or she might have had good reason. I don't know that I trust these men—"

I'd heard enough.

I was sure it was the same woman.

It all made so much sense now.

What she'd been hiding. Why she was really so afraid. Why she knew exactly how to touch us... please us... *manipulate* us. Lies. So many lies she'd woven, and we'd fallen for every one. I'd had my suspicions but pushed them away, instead of listening to my gut. I'd wanted to believe in her.

And she'd made William so damn happy.

I should have never let her sink her claws into him. I should have questioned her more that first day, should have trusted my instincts. I should have pushed her last night when she hadn't wanted to talk about Lord Carmichael. Ha! No wonder.

I wasn't going to make that mistake again. She was going to answer every last one of my questions.

"Careful, Clive!" The Sheriff had followed me out of the jail. "Don't do anything you'll regret."

I barked a laugh. It was a little too late for that. I'd let the little liar marry us without even properly questioning her.

Fury wrapped around me as I thundered out of town, galloping back to the ranch. This time, Sassy was going to tell me the truth.

―――

WILLIAM

I was on my horse when I saw Clive galloping down the road to the ranch, and worry rose up inside me. He wouldn't be rushing back like that unless something was wrong.

"I've got to go back to the house," I shouted to Jed, who'd been helping me repair the fence. "I'll be back."

Jed sent me a wave before going back to the fence, but I was already running for Blaze. Swinging myself into the saddle, I gave him a kick, and we leapt into action. Angling myself across the field, I let Blaze run flat out, giving him his head as he raced toward the house.

Clive's Thunder was bigger and slower, and the road wasn't as straight a shot as my path through the fields, so I managed to beat him by just a hair. Blaze danced in place, all worked up and happy after his little run.

"What's wrong?" I asked, breathless, jumping from Blaze's back. Clive's face was a thundercloud.

"She's a liar."

He spat the words, and it took me a moment to understand what he was saying, what he could mean.

"Hey!" I caught his arm when he made to move past me, spinning him back around. "Sassy? Our Sassy?"

Clive snorted. His dark eyes were burning with anger. Whatever he'd learned in town, he'd built up a full head of steam on his way back, and I wasn't going to let him approach Sassy when he was like this. She hadn't any experience dealing with an angry Clive, but I had plenty.

"She's not ours." He tried to shrug me off, but I held on tight and used his movement to push him back, setting myself protectively between him and the house.

"The hell, she isn't. What the hell happened in town?"

"There are men looking for her, but not for the reason she said," Clive said flatly. The lack of emotion in his voice wasn't good, not at all. It meant he barely had control of his temper and was right on the verge of erupting. "Get out of my way, William, I have some questions for our *wife*." He sneered at me on the final word.

Hell.

I stood my ground, clenching my fists. Even if Sassy had lied to us, even if not a word out of her mouth was true, that didn't mean she deserved Clive at his worst. Besides, we'd *seen* the kind of woman she was. Caring. Sensual. Eager for affection. Eager to bestow affection.

"You're not going in there 'til you tell me what's going on."

Maybe that would help shave off some of his anger. I didn't think he'd hurt her, not physically, but sometimes, Clive didn't realize how much damage he could do with his words.

"There's a man looking for her all right, her former lover. She was his mistress. And before that, she was a whore. She stole from him, assaulted him, and ran."

I stared at Clive.

Shit.

That... explained a lot, actually. At least about how she did things like easily suck our whole cocks down her throat, and why she didn't want to talk about her past. Had she been scared we'd reject her if we'd known? Clive and I weren't virgins, far from it, but there were different standards for men. It wouldn't have bothered me.

Was it bothering Clive?

"I don't care what she did before she came to us, she's

our wife now." I wasn't going back on that. If Clive intended to, we might have to part ways. The thought made me sick to my stomach, but I wasn't going to leave Sassy unprotected because of her past. Staying with Clive because he had some puritanical notion lodged in his head and leaving her in danger wouldn't just make me sick, I wouldn't be able to live with myself.

"You don't care that she lied?" Clive stared at me, flabbergasted.

"What does it matter what she did in the past? She's ours now, and she's a damn good wife," I shot back at him.

"But she *lied*. We don't know a thing about her, not really. She could be setting us up, just like she did him."

"Setting us up for what, Clive?" I swept my arm out, gesturing at the ranch. We had cows, horses she couldn't ride, a vegetable garden, chickens... "What do we have that she can physically steal? And where would she go with it? You aren't making a lick of sense."

He was starting to turn red in the face. Jabbing a finger at me, he scowled.

"No, you aren't making a lick of sense. She lied to us, and you don't even care. Or is it that you don't want to admit you were wrong about that damn ad?"

"I wasn't wrong!" Damnit. I shook my head. "That's not why, though, Clive. The ad doesn't matter. Her past doesn't matter. You aren't thinking straight."

"No, *you* aren't thinking straight. You've got her built up in your head to be something she's not, and you aren't willing to admit she's not perfect because that would ruin the happy little dream you've concocted. I knew something was wrong from the start, but I kept stepping back, trying to give you what you wanted—"

"Oh, sure, *giving* me what I wanted," I cut off his tirade, shaking my head. My fists flexed. That was pure Clive. Now that he thought marrying Sassy was a mistake, it was all *my* fault. Not that I agreed with him about it being a mistake, but my temper was soaring. "Because sharing a wife was some great sacrifice on your part, you've been suffering terribly—"

"It doesn't matter." He slashed his hand through the air as if that would be the end of the argument. "I'm going in to ask her some questions, and this time, she *is* going to answer." He stepped forward, but I didn't move. I braced myself, feet apart, muscles tensed, and head lowered.

"Like hell. You want to question *our* wife, you'll have to go through me first."

"Don't do this, William," Clive warned, taking another step toward me, his dark eyes glinting with barely repressed violence. "I don't want to hurt you."

Arrogant bastard. Of course, he assumed he'd win in a fight.

"Then turn around and walk away until you come to your senses," I snapped back.

"Why the hell are you still defending that lying whore?" he snarled.

That did it. Lunging forward, I slammed my fist into his chin.

11

WHY THE HELL are you still defending that lying whore?

I stood frozen on the side of the house, heart pounding and tears welling, Clive's vicious question echoing in my head. I'd been in the garden and had come back to the house when I'd heard raised voices. When I got to the back of the house, I'd recognized Clive's and William's voices and heard what they were saying.

Knew *they* knew.

Knew William either didn't care or was hiding it from himself that he did.

Knew Clive cared deeply. That he felt betrayed. Lied to. And he should. I had done both, hadn't I? Now, I'd set them against each other, without even meaning to, and I could hear them fighting. Hear the grunts of pain, fists slamming against flesh.

I should have run out there and tried to stop them. I should have accepted whatever castigation Clive wanted to heap on me. I should have told them I wasn't worth fighting over, and Clive was right.

But I couldn't face them.

Couldn't bear to see Clive turn away from me.

Couldn't bear to see if William looked at me differently, despite his words.

Couldn't bear to see them fighting because of me.

So, I did what came naturally—I turned tail and ran. Ran past the henhouse and the vegetable garden, past the well, and over the hill, until I couldn't hear them anymore, then fell to my knees, sobbing as though my heart was breaking... because it was.

Had I really thought I would be able to hide my past from them forever?

Had I really thought they would accept my past?

William didn't seem bothered, a little voice whispered in my head. It didn't matter, though. It clearly bothered Clive, and he and William were partners. They'd been partners for far longer than they'd known me. I would never expect William to choose me over Clive, wouldn't even want him to. The two of them needed each other, balanced each other.

I had just hoped I could be part of that balance, had thought maybe they would come to love me the way I already loved them.

But it was too soon, far too soon to hope any feelings they did have for me could last in the face of my past.

Thief.

Whore.

I could not deny the charges. I was both.

I was also a woman who had fallen in love. It didn't matter I had not known them long, I'd fallen in love with both of them. Had thought I might have even found happiness with them.

I should have known better.

Since when had any part of my life ended happily?

Slowly, my tears ran out, leaving me drained. Empty. Hopeless.

My knees were beginning to hurt, the ground hard and rocky under my skirts, but I had not noticed until now. I slowly got to my feet, staring off into the distance, the endless fields...

I could keep running.

It wasn't Lord Carmichael I wanted to run from, though, it was my husbands. My husbands who deserved an apology from me, at the very least, even if they were unlikely to remain my husbands for much longer. They should know I was sorry for deceiving them.

Sorry for coming between them.

I did not expect it to change how Clive felt about me, but he still deserved to hear it. And William... my sweet, gentle William, my defender, even when he shouldn't have. I didn't know how to make it up to him, but I could at least try to explain. They deserved to hear the truth from me.

What happened after that... well, it didn't matter. Nothing felt like it mattered now. I would do whatever they wished of me.

Weary but resolute, I turned around.

A man was standing there, one I had never seen before, and my eyes widened when he grinned at me. It was not a nice grin.

"There ye are," he said, his accent clearly British.

I screamed and turned to run, but it was too late. Something slammed into the back of my head, and everything went dark.

———

Clive

WHEN HAD William become so brawny?

I'd wanted to be careful not to hurt him, but within seconds, I was fighting in earnest, the only way to keep him from walloping me.

My jaw was aching from his first punch, my gut from his second, but I'd managed to dodge the third and give him a good one in his side. He was faster, though, and I quickly realized I wasn't going to be able to lay him out the way I'd thought. My best chance was to take him to the ground and use my heavier bulk to keep him there.

Launching myself at him, I slammed my shoulder into his middle, tackling him to the ground. William shouted his outrage as he went down, twisting and taking me with him. We rolled along the ground, kicking up dust as we grappled for supremacy.

"Stay down!" I growled, bracing my arm across his chest, but he didn't listen.

He threw me off and dove for me, then we rolled again, dangerously close to the horses, who started to dance, hooves flashing. That brought us both back to our senses. It was one thing to wrestle with each other, but if we spooked the horses, we were both liable to be trampled, then where would we be?

Panting, we broke apart, scrambling back from Blaze and Thunder, who eyed us nervously, still shifting their weight. We eyed each other. I rubbed my jaw, wincing when I hit a sore spot. William probed his ribs, hissing when he touched where I'd landed a punch.

A lot of the anger I'd carried with me all the way home was gone. Instead of being a ball of rage, it had dropped to a low simmer, and I was already starting to feel ashamed of some of the things I said. I had a temper and knew it, but it always ran hot and was over with just as quickly.

I was grateful Sassy hadn't been around to hear it. I glanced at the house, which wasn't that far away from us. At least, I hoped she hadn't heard me. I wasn't sure how loud I'd been. I'd been so worked up...

"Feeling better now?" William asked, rolling his head

around his neck and clapping his hands against his chaps to get some of the dust off.

"A bit," I admitted. "I still want to know why she lied to us, though." I didn't like lies. Once someone started lying about little things, it was easier to lie about big things. That was one of the reasons I'd partnered up with William—the man was honest as the day was long and utterly incapable of subterfuge.

"If you call her a lying whore again, we're going to do this all over," he warned, sending a flinty look my way, his blue eyes hard.

I winced. "I didn't mean it like that."

Not really.

"Good. I don't care if she was a whore. As far as I'm concerned, we've been reaping the benefits of her experience." A little smile kicked up on the side of his face.

That was one way of looking at it.

"What if she's been faking her pleasure?" I didn't like the insecurities now niggling at me, and that one was at the top of the heap. William and I had both been strutting around like roosters with our erotic prowess. What if it had all been false?

"Then she is the greatest actress in the world," William said with a snort, not bothering to hide his contempt for the idea. "What does your gut tell you?"

That her body's responses were honest, even if she hadn't been. I sighed, getting to my feet and dusting myself off.

"She still lied." I clung stubbornly to the fact that bothered me the most.

"We'll spank her ass and tell her she's not to do it again," William said, following me to his feet. "I don't think she's lied about anything else. She's avoided talking about it. I don't think she likes lying to us."

As usual, I thought William was taking a rosy view of the situation, but for the first time, my cynical self wanted to believe. I didn't want everything we'd been building with Sassy to have been false. I wanted her...

I wanted her to care as much about us as we did about her.

I wanted her to love us—to love me, the same way I loved her.

That's why I'd been so damn angry. I'd gone and fallen in love with my wife and couldn't be sure she felt the same way. Couldn't be sure she should be trusted, even if she said she did, and the uncertainty made my stomach churn.

It was easier to be angry than hurt.

"We should find her and ask some questions," I said firmly. "Then she's definitely getting a spanking." William nodded his agreement, but before we could move, we heard the whinny of a horse, and movement out of the corner of my eye caught my attention.

Both of our heads whipped around to see a man on horseback, galloping away through the fields, something big draped over his lap.

WILLIAM

"Sassy!" I called out her name before I could think, taking a step forward as if I could somehow bring her back to us with just her name.

The horseman was riding away with her over his lap —I recognized the fabric of her dress—and I doubted either of them could hear us if she was even conscious. From the way her body was flopping, I doubted it. Fear seized my heart, freezing my chest.

"Damn!" Clive spat out the curse, but unlike me, he didn't freeze, leaping into motion. I followed him, only a moment behind. It took us precious seconds to free Thunder and Blaze from where we'd hitched them to the fence post and get them turned in the right direction.

Precious seconds to follow the unknown horseman.

Thankfully, the land was flat, and we could see him, even if he was just a tiny silhouette on the horizon. I clenched my jaw with anger as I saw the way Sassy's legs, arms, and head were flopping. She *must* be unconscious. He was going to pay for that.

We'd promised to protect and cherish her, and today, we were failing on both fronts.

We followed him for several miles to a break in our fence, which had Clive and me exchanging hard looks. That was new. I'd just walked this line last week. It was damn lucky we hadn't lost any cattle through it, although part of me was grateful the horseman hadn't had to jump the fence with Sassy perched so precariously on his lap.

About a mile off our lands, near the river, we could see a campsite ahead. Smoke came from the fire, and the horseman with Sassy had slowed to a walk.

I grit my teeth, watching as two men jumped up to help lift her down from her kidnapper. They were touching our wife... none too gently either. As we came closer, I could see her head lolling.

One of the men was already backing away, holding onto her, while her kidnapper and the other man turned to face us, hands on their holsters. I don't know why they didn't draw, but they were going to regret not taking us seriously as a threat. Clive and I were damn fast with our draws, and these two didn't look comfortable in their stances. We got down from Blaze and Thunder, stepping in front of them. The horses snorted but didn't move.

A fourth man, one I hadn't noticed until we were almost upon them, stood up next to the fire as Clive and I came to a halt about fifteen feet away. The man holding Sassy had stepped back beside the man next to the fire, so he could see her face.

Dark-haired and tall, his handsome face was ruined by a vicious red scar that ran across his entire face. His eye on that side was damaged. Whoever slashed him had gotten him right across it.

"That's her," he said, his voice filled with anger and satisfaction. His accent was different from Sassy's, that of an English lord rather than a commoner. This had to be Lord Carmichael, come all the way from England to find her.

Remembering what Clive had said about her assaulting the man, I could only guess she'd been the one to give him the scar across his face. He hadn't just been hunting her because he'd wanted her... he likely wanted revenge.

"That's our wife," Clive said coldly, making Carmichael finally turn to look at us.

His lip curled up in a sneer as he looked us over, clearly unimpressed.

"Then you should be thanking me for taking this whore off your hands." He barked a short laugh. "Although I shouldn't be surprised, a harlot like her would end up with two husbands. Apparently, she could only change her ways so far."

Anger bubbled up in my gut, roiling and seething, and if I could have done so without endangering Sassy, I would have thrown myself at him right then.

"He said, that's our wife," I responded, my tone lethal. "Give her back to us, and we'll let you go quietly and forget your insults to her."

The lord's eyes widened with incredulity. "Are you threatening me?"

It had taken him long enough to notice.

12

VOICES STIRRED through the darkness as my throbbing head drew me back to consciousness.

"I admit she's a good fuck, gentlemen, but she's hardly worth dying over."

I recognized that voice, and it filled me with horror and despair. My head throbbed harder, and I fought back a whimper. Maybe if I could fall back into unconsciousness, I'd awaken again to find this was all a dream.

"I'm glad you feel that way." That was Clive's rough voice. Clive was here for me? Even though... even though... Anguish filled me as I remembered his anger, his fight with William. That hurt even more than my head did. "Hand her over, and you won't have to die."

"Has it escaped your notice that you're outnumbered?" Lord Carmichael's voice hardened, and my breath caught in my throat. Oh, God... my husbands were going to be killed, and it was all my fault.

My eyes popped open as I began to struggle against the arms holding me. I was unceremoniously dropped onto the ground, knocking the breath from me. The sight that met my eyes did nothing to make me feel better.

William and Clive were both there, hands on their holsters, glaring daggers at the two men standing in front of me. I could see my husbands through their legs. I glanced up to see Carmichael on my right, glaring at my husbands. Carmichael's face was horrifically scarred, and I gasped when I saw my handiwork, jerking my gaze away. Twisting my head around, there was another unknown man standing behind me, blocking off any chance of escape.

I peeked at Carmichael again.

No wonder he'd chased me across the ocean and into the west. I had ruined his face and one of his eyes. Likely ruined his chances of a good marriage. How would he have explained such a scar? Most women of the *ton* would have run screaming at the sight, although there would likely have been those who would hold their noses for his title... though he wouldn't have wanted to marry any of the latter.

He'd been one of most handsome men in England, and I'd taken that from him. I'd done more than reject him and steal from him—I'd taken away his face.

He was here for revenge.

None of the men looked at me, not even Carmichael, disregarding me as unimportant. They were all focused on William and Clive, who both snorted at Lord Carmichael's words.

"Last warning," Clive said, glaring at Lord Carmichael. I clapped my hands over my mouth, not wanting to distract them.

"Kill them," Lord Carmichael snarled. I screamed as rough fingers grabbed my hair, pulling upward. The pain in my head intensified, my scalp burning, and I lashed out, kicking hard as the sound of gunshots filled the air.

Oh God, they're dead, and it's all my fault.

Tears burned my eyes, from more than the pain, and I found Carmichael's hand in my hair. I grabbed onto him, digging in my nails, kicking and screaming for all I was worth.

I knew he meant to kill me, too, but I wasn't going to make it easy for him. I felt my foot connect and dug in my nails harder, sinking them into the flesh of his hand, scratching like a hellcat.

I heard him bellow, then felt the blow across my face that left my ears ringing.

Another shout, more gunshots, horses whinnied, and more shouting. I couldn't take in the words, couldn't make sense of them. Everything was too chaotic. There was so much dust, and my eyes were full of tears, even though I hadn't thought I had any left.

I kicked and kicked and kicked. Arms wrapped

around me from behind, and I screamed so loud, it hurt my throat.

"Let go, Sassy, let go, sweetheart, I've got you," William said in my ear, gentle, soothing.

I sank back against him, sobbing and blinking, only now realizing Lord Carmichael's grip on my hair had loosened. William rocked back, pulling me onto his lap and holding me in his arms. I clung to him, selfishly taking in every drop of comfort he offered, even though I knew I didn't deserve it.

The sound of fighting drew my gaze, and my eyes widened. The two men who had been standing in front of me were dead on the ground, blood stains on their chest. I couldn't see them very well, they were too far away from me, but I could tell they weren't moving. Just past them, Clive was rolling around with the man who had been standing behind me.

"Clive!" I whispered his name, jerking forward, but William held me back.

"Stop that, sweetheart. He's enjoying himself." William tightened his arms around me. "He's got quite a bit of anger to work out."

I didn't understand. I didn't understand any of this. How was this possible?

"Well, these guys seem more used to fists than pistols," William told me, which was when I realized I'd asked the question aloud. "Clive and I got the draw on them, then I shot Carmichael while he was trying to drag you up in front of him as a shield." His tone gave

Carmichael's title a sardonic twist. "Clive decided to jump on the last henchman and work out some of his issues, instead of shooting him, I suppose."

"He's dead?" I twisted around on William's lap. Deep down, some part of me knew Carmichael was dead, or William wouldn't be holding me, but I had to see for myself.

William tried to stop me from looking. "Sweetheart, don't—"

"No, I need to see him," I whispered, pushing his hand away from my face. "I need to see it for myself, William, or I'll never believe it. Not deep down."

He sighed but let me look.

I almost gasped again. I hadn't realized Carmichael's body was so close to us, only a few feet away. He was lying on his back, eyes wide open and sightless, staring at the sky. There were two holes in his chest, and blood trickled from the corner of his mouth.

Definitely dead.

The sight both unnerved and reassured me. I buried my face in William's chest, almost wishing I hadn't looked. Guilt welled at being reassured by a man's death, even though I knew he wouldn't have felt an ounce, causing mine or my husbands' death, had the tables been turned. I didn't like knowing I was the reason *anyone* had died.

Muttering a curse low, under his breath, William shifted around, his arms tightening around me as he got to his feet, easily lifting me.

"Clive, stop playing with him," William barked out the command. "We need to get the Sheriff here."

A new fear gripped my heart, and I lifted my head again.

"The Sheriff?" The question came out in a worried whisper, my throat too tight to speak any louder. "Aren't you going to be in trouble for... for..."

Three dead men and one beaten into submission. Clive stood over the man he'd just been brawling with, tying his hands behind his back. If he and William faced any consequences, that would be my fault as well.

Why couldn't I do anything right?

I was breathing faster, yet couldn't get enough air, as if an iron band was squeezing my chest so tightly, I couldn't really get a full breath. William gave me a little shake.

"Breathe, sweetheart. Everything's going to be fine."

Closing my eyes, I leaned my head against his shoulder and whimpered. The pounding in my head returned with a vengeance as if someone was hammering on the inside of my skull.

"Sassy? Sassy, what's wrong?" William sounded panicked.

"My head hurts." I whimpered again, then everything went dark.

———

Clive

. . .

"Looks like he hit her good on the back of the head, but she should be fine after a couple day's rest," Doc said, packing up his kit. "All her other injuries are minor."

William and I both breathed a sigh of relief, relaxing for the first time since Sassy had passed out in William's arms. I'd taken her back home while William had raced to fetch the doc and the sheriff.

She looked so pale and small, lying in the middle of our big bed, lips tightened with pain.

"If the pain gets to be too much, give her a couple drops of this with some water." Doc handed me a small glass bottle with a stopper. I curled my fingers around it, holding onto it as though it was precious. It kind of was, wasn't it? I couldn't stand the idea of Sassy in pain.

"Thanks, Doc," William said, clapping the man on the shoulder. "We appreciate you checking her over."

"Of course." Doc glanced at her again and shook his head. "I hate to see one of our women laid low, but I can tell she's a fighter."

I chuckled. "You should see the other guys."

If Sassy hadn't started screaming and fighting, things wouldn't have gone quite as easily. She'd distracted Carmichael and his last hired hand, making it a lot easier for William and me to take them down when we could have easily been shot instead.

Doc snorted. "So, I heard. I believe I have an appointment to see one of them in the jail when I'm done here." He gave me a look.

I shrugged. I had no regrets. I'd had a lot of anger to

work out. The man was still alive, wasn't he? That was more than the others could say. We'd had to even the odds.

"When will she wake up?" William asked, still worried.

"Oh, anytime now, I'd say." Doc nodded reassuringly. "It could be five minutes, it could be an hour. She's had quite a day."

Yes, she had. She was battered and bruised all over. My lips tightened, and I wished Carmichael's death hadn't been so quick. He'd deserved to suffer more. If I could have given him a bruise to match every one of Sassy's...

But he was gone, and she wouldn't have to be afraid, no threat hanging over her head.

We still needed to deal with her dishonesty, but not until she was fully recovered. My cock tried to rise when I thought about spanking her perfectly rounded ass until she was very sorry, she'd ever lied, but I pushed back the thought. That was days away.

Doc left, and William and I sat down on either side of the bed, each holding one of Sassy's hands and watching her pale face for any sign of movement.

"We're going to have to get back to the ranch, eventually," I murmured unhappily. We both wanted to take care of her, but part of that included taking care of the ranch. If our source of income fell apart, we would all suffer. Yet leaving our wife alone when she was injured felt plain wrong.

William nodded reluctantly. "We could trade off. Just for the rest of today and tomorrow. See how she's doing after that."

Sassy stirred, causing us to fall silent. Sitting up alertly, we waited to see what happened. Her lips parted, her eyelashes fluttered, and a little moan escaped. William and I squeezed her hands, giving her whatever comfort we could.

"It's okay, sweetheart, just relax, you're safe," William said soothingly. To my surprise, she did relax as soon as she heard his voice. I was glad he was there. I hadn't even considered she might wake confused, not realizing she was safe.

Slowly, her eyes opened, and she focused on us, one after the other.

"Lord Carmichael is dead?"

"As a doornail," I said quickly. Her eyes widened, and William coughed. Damn, might have been too crass. "How's your head? The Doc left some medicine if it hurts too much."

"It's okay." She winced, wrinkling her nose as though she wasn't sure of what she'd just said. "I think. It doesn't hurt as much as it did... it..." Her voice trailed off, eyes shifting, then she tried to jerk her hand back. I tightened my grip, and she stared up at me. "Why are you being so nice to me?"

I frowned. "Why wouldn't I be nice?"

To my horror, tears sprung to her eyes.

"You... you were so angry. You called me... you called

me a... lying whore." Her voice dropped, whispering the last two words, and my heart dropped as well.

I hadn't realized she'd heard that. Shame filled me, and I hung my head, but I didn't let go of her hand—I couldn't.

"I'm sorry, sweetheart, I was angry that you'd lied to us, but I should have *never* said that, never called you that."

"He's got a temper, but it moves fast," William said, also sounding apologetic on my behalf. "He says things he doesn't mean sometimes."

"I'm working on it," I added hastily. I was never going to call her that again. Just the hurt look in her eyes made my heart ache. "If I forget again, William will pop me a good one."

Instead of smiling, her lips tightened. "I didn't like you two fighting. Not over me. I'm not worth it."

Both of us scowled down at her.

"The hell you aren't," I said.

"Yes, you are," William said, right over top of me. "You're worth everything, Sassy."

The expression on her face was disbelieving, which made me scowl even harder.

"I don't care that you lied to us. I mean, I do care, and we're going to discuss that later," I quickly amended, "but it doesn't change how I feel about you."

"How you feel about me?" Her eyes widened again.

"I love you." There, I'd said it. Something inside me eased once I had the words out. I'd never said them to a woman, other than my mother, but it felt right... because it was. Sassy was my wife. I was still ticked she'd lied to us, but my anger didn't diminish my feelings.

"And I love you," William said, right on top of my confession.

Sassy's eyes filled with tears, and her hand squeezed mine tight.

13

"HOW... HOW CAN THIS BE POSSIBLE?" I wanted to believe them, I wanted to believe them *so badly*, but it didn't make any sense.

They knew what I was, what I had been... how could they possibly *love* me?

"How could we not?" William asked, a small smile curving his lips. "Why wouldn't we?"

Clive's grin was a little lopsided. Despite his words earlier, I could see how sincere he'd been in his apology. Their hands were warm around mine, comforting, and neither of them was willing to let go.

"I was a whore," I said baldly, bitterly, watching them

for any change in their expression, but they just stared back.

"And now, you're our wife," Clive said, finality in his tone. "Are you planning on returning to being a whore?"

"No!"

"Are you going to go looking for pleasure with other men for the fun of it?" William asked.

"No!" I would have shaken my head, but the smallest movement sent a little jab of pain through my skull, and I immediately stilled. Both of them were already leaning forward, looking at me closely.

"Are you alright?"

"Don't shake your head like that, sweetheart."

My lips pressed together as a sob rose in my chest. They settled back into their places on the bed, steadily regarding me. Did my past really not matter to them? It had seemed to matter a great deal to Clive.

I met his gaze. "Why were you so angry before then? Why aren't you still angry?"

"I wasn't angry that you were a whore," he said, then paused. "I wish it hadn't been necessary for you to become one, but I wasn't angry. I was angry, you lied."

"He has a thing about lies," William said.

"I don't trust easily," Clive admitted. "So, when I do and find out I was lied to, it hurts. It makes me wonder what else the person lied about, and when the person is someone I love..." His voice trailed off, and then he shrugged. "I started to wonder if everything you'd said to us was a lie."

"No!" I squeezed his hand tight. Out of all the possibilities, that had not been one I'd considered. "I'm so sorry... I never... I never meant to hurt you." I hadn't really thought I could.

"We know, sweetheart," William said sympathetically. "You'll be punished for lying, and that will wipe the slate clean, and we can start over."

"P-p-punished?" That was the last thing I expected to hear, especially from my sweet William. Usually, Clive was the threatening one, although he'd never made me feel unsafe. Even when he'd been mad and yelling insults, I hadn't feared he'd physically hurt me.

But 'punishment' sounded very ominous.

"We would never harm you, Sassy," Clive said seriously, his thumb stroking over my hand. "But we are going to spank you for lying to us."

"Spank me?" Like a child? Put me over their laps and use their hands to smack my upturned bottom? Heat rose in my cheeks when the image that flashed through my mind caused a very *odd* and unexpected reaction in my body.

"Spank you," William confirmed.

"But that will hurt," I protested, not at all sure how I felt about this turn of events.

A part of me was intrigued by the idea, but another part was repelled. I trusted my husbands not to *really* hurt me, but that didn't mean I liked the idea—at least, most of me didn't. And I was not at all comfortable with the part of me becoming aroused while thinking about being *spanked*, of all things.

After being kidnapped, threatened, seeing my husbands have to kill to save us all, and then fainting, how could I possibly be aroused? Especially by the idea of being *spanked*?

"It will hurt, yes." Clive's gaze turned stern. "The next time you think about lying, you'll remember that it hurt, and it wasn't worth doing."

I hunched my shoulders on the pillow. "I wasn't going to again, anyway," I muttered.

"Glad to hear it," Clive said, giving my hand another little squeeze. "But you'll still be punished."

William nodded his agreement, and I sighed. I certainly couldn't fight both of them.

"Now," Clive said, pinning me with his gaze. "I want you to tell us everything."

So, I did. I didn't give them specific details, but I told them about my father's death, my vain attempts to find a job in London, Mrs. Burk finding and rescuing me—both of them tensed at my description, but that's what she had done. I could have ended up with a far worse fate. Of course, she eventually betrayed me, but before that, she *had* saved me.

I told them about befriending the other women in Mrs. Burk's house and how I'd become comfortable there. I told them about Lord Carmichael's initial interest in me and the rumors about the woman who had disappeared with him. I told them about fighting him off and my escape to the docks, using the money I stole from him to buy my passage on a boat to New York, then finding my new housing and a factory job once I was there. And finally, about my fears, Carmichael would follow and my relief when I'd seen their ad.

Then my two men laid down on either side, holding me until I fell back asleep, feeling completely and utterly safe.

————

WILLIAM

THE NEXT FEW days weren't easy on any of us. The Sheriff had to do a thorough report, which took both Clive and me away from the ranch on the first day we were already taking turns staying with Sassy. She finally shooed us away, insisting she was well enough to take care of herself during the day, even though we forbade her from doing any strenuous housework.

I thought Clive was going to spank her right then and there, the day we came home to find she'd done the wash.

"It wasn't that difficult," Sassy protested, backing away with her hands over her bottom, a pretty flush rising in her cheeks. "I took it in small loads, so I didn't have to carry anything heavy."

"Which meant it took longer than usual when you should have been resting," Clive retorted, his arms crossed over his chest. I leaned against the kitchen table, thoughtfully watching our wife.

She had recovered quickly, even though Clive and I worried. My cock ached as I stared at her. We hadn't made love to her since she'd been kidnapped, too worried about the knock to her head and the various bruises she'd been dealt. Most of those were already healing, though, and so was her head.

As far as I knew, she hadn't had a single headache the past two days.

Sassy groaned. "I'm tired of resting, Clive. I need to *do* something with my time, or I'll go mad."

"You could have dusted or something," Clive said, taking another step toward her. Sassy rolled her eyes, likely because she'd spent the day before yesterday, dusting. The house was already about as clean as it could get, and all our mending was done. What we had been short on were clean clothes. "Don't roll your eyes at me, wife, or I'll put you over my knee right now."

Sassy wrinkled her nose at him.

"If I can't handle doing the laundry, I certainly can't handle being spanked," she retorted.

"I agree," I said, startling both of them. Clive's head whipped around, a frown descending on his brow, while Sassy's eyes went wide. She was just as startled as Clive.

"You do?" They both asked at the same time, albeit with different inflections.

"I do." I straightened up, a slow grin spreading on my face. "But since Sassy clearly was able to handle doing the laundry, she should also be able to handle being spanked. Which means it's time we discussed her lying."

"That's not what I meant!" Sassy squeaked, backing up another step.

"You can't have it both ways, sweetheart," Clive said, crossing his arms over his chest.

"Well, neither can you," she sassed back, fully living up to her name. "You don't think I'm fit enough to do laundry; therefore, I can't be fit enough for a spanking."

"A compromise then," I said. "We'll give you this evening and tomorrow to rest, then spank you tomorrow night."

"Sounds fair." Clive grinned. "Don't you think so, Sassy?"

Her mouth dropped open. "You want me to agree to my own spanking?"

"Of course." I raised an eyebrow at her. "There's no point in punishing you unless you accept that you deserve it and want to change your ways. So, since you feel fit enough to have done the laundry today, will you be ready to accept your punishment tomorrow for lying to us?"

Cheeks turning pink, Sassy's gaze slid away from mine, her head dropping down, and she nodded—a short, quick nod, but she agreed. Satisfaction rose up inside me.

"Good girl," I said, walking forward. This time, she didn't retreat. Cupping her chin, I tilted her head back for a kiss.

"Very good girl," Clive agreed as my lips pressed against hers. I could feel him coming up to my side, watching as my lips moved over hers.

We'd been so gentle with her, waiting for her to recover, barely doing more than brush her lips with our own. This time was different. If Sassy felt well enough to start taking on some of the more arduous household chores, she was certainly well enough for a more energetic kiss.

My cock thickened as I plundered her mouth, kissing her with all the pent-up fervor that had built up over the past few days.

Clive agreed. As soon as I released Sassy, he swept her up, kissing her just as thoroughly and leaving her panting. Her eyes sparkled when he finally let her go, and I could see the hard nubs of her nipples pressing against her dress. Hell, I wanted her so bad... but we needed to wait.

That was something else Clive and I had discussed. The next time we took Sassy to bed, we wanted to claim her—fully.

"If she's getting a spanking tomorrow, I think she needs the plug tonight." My already hard cock throbbed with approval. Sassy groaned as Clive nodded his agreement.

———

SASSY

. . .

BENT OVER THE KITCHEN TABLE, my skirts up around my hips, I whimpered as two slick fingers pushed into my backside. The tight little hole stretched open, the slight burn of being filled, making me squirm in discomfort.

"Why do I need a plug if I'm getting a spanking?" I asked plaintively.

My husbands had handled me like glass the past few days, and while at first, I had appreciated their thoughtfulness, today, I had gotten antsy for more than soft kisses and light caresses. I wanted to feel them again. I had thought doing the laundry would show them I was feeling much better, but that hadn't gone quite the way I'd thought it would.

The fingers inside me twisted, and my breath hitched, pleasure sliding through me at the sensation. Having my bottom played with, instead of my pussy, was an awful tease, especially after so many days without any sexual satisfaction. I wanted *them*, not the plug.

"Oh, the plug isn't for the spanking, not really," William said, moving his fingers back and forth in my ass. I gasped, pussy clenching as he fucked my bottom with the thick digits, mimicking the sex act. "It's for what we're going to do after."

Fingers gripped my hair, right at the base of my skull, and Clive tugged, pulling my head back, so he could look at me. His dark eyes were full of lustful promise.

"Tomorrow, sweetheart, we're going to spank you and

wipe the slate clean. And once we have that nice, clean slate, we're going to claim you."

"I'm going to fuck your sweet pussy." William picked up the thread of conversation from Clive, his fingers still moving inside of me, propelling my arousal to new heights. "And Clive is going to fuck this lovely ass."

"So, you need the plug to prepare," Clive finished, lowering his lips to mine for a ruthless kiss that left me reeling almost as much as the vivid picture they painted.

William's fingers withdrew, then I felt the hard nose of the plug pushing into me. I moaned, my eyes fluttering shut against Clive's intense gaze. I could feel him watching me, documenting every tiny change in my expression as William pumped the plug back and forth, forcing my bottom open wider and wider until I cried out as the widest part of the plug breached my entrance.

The sharp pain was over almost as soon as it began, the rest of the plug easily pushing inside. I shuddered. It felt huge. I didn't know if they'd used a larger plug, or if it just felt that way because I had gone so many days without it, but it felt much larger than I remembered. I panted for breath as Clive slowly lowered my head down to the table.

William's fingers swept through the slick folds of my pussy, and my hips jerked, but he pulled away before I could begin to enjoy the stimulation.

Leaning over me, he whispered in my ear, "Tomorrow, sweetheart."

14

I DON'T THINK William and I had ever worked so damn fast in our lives. Both of us knew what was waiting for us at the end of the day, and neither of us wanted to wait one moment longer than we had to before we could punish and claim our wife. We stopped by the creek on the way home to quickly scrub ourselves clean, changing into the clothing we'd packed in our saddlebags. It was an extra effort and a small delay, but tonight was a special night.

Sassy was waiting for us when we walked into the house, her head coming up, then ducking back down as she bent over the stew simmering on the stove.

"What, no greeting?" William teased. Normally, she

jumped up to greet us. We knew why she was feeling more uncomfortable today, but it was still amusing.

"I... yes, of course." Flushing bright red, Sassy hurried forward to give us our kisses, William first, then me.

William crowded in behind her, his hands sliding down her back to her bottom as I kissed her, making her squeak and squirm between us. My cock was already achingly hard. Pressing her softness against me, I claimed her mouth, kissing her deeply and thoroughly. Then I released her, turning her back around to face William for another kiss, so I could caress her as I undid the buttons on her dress. We passed her back and forth between us, stripping her down and stealing her breath with kisses.

I cupped her breast, pinching her nipple and making her moan against William's lips. He slid his hand between her legs, stroking her wetness as she gasped against mine.

Once she was completely naked, I spun her back around to kiss William again, while I settled onto one of the chairs, watching and waiting. My hand was already itchy with anticipation, my cock throbbing and waiting. When he turned her around, she turned bright red when she saw me sitting there, and her head ducked down again.

"Time for your punishment," I said sternly, patting my thigh. "Come here and put yourself over my lap, Sassy."

She hesitated, but William took her hand and led her over, helping her bend, so her bottom was high in the air. My hand rested on that pretty curve of flesh, fingertips almost touching the flat base of the plug buried between her cheeks. The bulge of my cock pressed against her side, and she squirmed against it, rubbing the thick length through my pants, and making me groan.

"Do you understand why you're being punished, Sassy?" William asked, rubbing the small of her back.

Sassy turned her head to look at him, her voice quivering.

"Because I lied. I'm so sorry. I thought you wouldn't marry me if you knew."

"I can understand that," I said, patting her bottom gently. "But after we were married, I'd like to think you were getting to know us well enough to trust us."

"I..." Her voice trailed off before returning, more tearfully. "I'm sorry."

"We know, sweetheart," William said.

"Now, I'm going to give you something to think about the next time you're tempted to tell a lie." Raising my hand, I brought it down on her bottom, hard enough to sting.

———

Sassy

"Ow!" I jerked against Clive's legs, but there was more surprise in my voice than pain. My bottom clenching around the plug was more uncomfortable than the swat that had just landed on my upturned cheeks.

Clive's hand came down again and again with short, crisp swats that stung when they landed, but the sensation quickly morphed into a general warmth until another swat slapped against my skin. I squirmed, panting as my bottom heated.

This wasn't so bad. Not really. In fact, it was rather arousing. Something about being over Clive's lap, my side pressed against his hard cock, his hand coming down on my ass, and William watching from behind, made me all achy and needy. Or maybe it was because I knew what was coming after this. My pussy pulsed in anticipation.

"That's a nice rosy pink hue," William said admiringly, and I blushed, thankful they couldn't see my face. "Her pussy is nice and slick, too. I think she's enjoying this."

"Then I guess we can be done with the warmup," Clive said.

Wait... warmup?

The next swat made me shriek, my body jerking upright, but both men's hands pushed my upper body back down, so Clive could land another hard swat to my backside. These swats didn't sting, they *burned*, little explosions of fire every time Clive's hand landed.

"Ow! Ow! I'm sorry! Oh, please, I'm sorry. I won't do it again!"

With their hands holding me in place, I could do no more than squirm and shriek apologies as my bottom cheeks went from warm and tingly to fiery hot and throbbing under Clive's firm hand. My legs kicked, and tears slid down my cheeks.

I *should* have trusted them.

I wished I *had* trusted them.

I wished I had been the one to tell them about my past. To *show* them how much I loved them. To let them show me how much they loved me.

I began to sob in earnest, Clive's hand beating out a rapid tattoo on my bottom, but it didn't feel the same as when I'd cried after seeing him and William fight. These weren't guilt-ridden tears of anguish. They were freeing tears of absolution—acknowledging the frightened girl I'd been, the frightened young woman I'd turned into, and finally, the strong woman I'd become—a woman who loved her husbands and was loved in return. Despite the seared state of my buttocks, I felt nothing but relief and joy... well, emotionally, at least.

The spanking finally stopped, leaving me limp over Clive's lap, my bottom pulsating from the painful blaze his hand had ignited. I was lifted upright, wincing when my sore, throbbing cheeks touched the rough fabric of his pants.

"It's all done, Sassy," Clive said soothingly.

"You took your punishment so well," William praised, kneeling beside us, so he could hold me from the other side.

"I love you." The words blurted out of me, unable to hold them back any longer. "I love you both so much. I'm so sorry I didn't trust you before, or I did, but I didn't act like it—"

"Shh, shh," they cut me off, soothing me.

"Slate's wiped clean, remember?" William smiled and leaned forward to kiss my tear-stained cheek. "Now, then. I think we should move on to the next part of our evening."

"Dinner?" Clive asked. "That stew smells good." I giggled, and William scowled at him. Clive's sense of humor came out at the oddest times.

"Please," I said, winding my arms about Clive's neck. "I want you both."

"As my lady wishes," Clive said, standing with me in his arms. William grinned and darted in front of us, heading for the bedroom. He had the door open and disappeared inside, and by the time we entered, he was already stripping down.

My bottom was still fiery and hot, but some of that heat had made its way to my core, burning me up on the inside. Just looking at William's hard body and erect cock made my pussy clench. He grinned wickedly at me and laid down on the bed, one hand on his cock, and the other reaching out to me, beckoning me. Clive set me down on my feet and gave my bottom a little slap that made me shriek.

Any other time, I would have barely felt it, but right now, my ass was extra sensitive.

"Come here, beautiful," William said, reaching for me. "I want you on my cock."

I wanted to be on his cock.

Walking to the bed, I took his hand, pausing only long enough to bend my head and give the head of his cock a kiss before climbing onto the bed and straddling him. My breasts hung down in his face, and he immediately reached up to plump them as I positioned myself above his cock. I moaned when he pinched my nipples as he tugged me downward, sending little tingles of pleasure running through my body.

Out of the corner of my eye, I could see Clive watching us as he slowly stripped down. Throwing my head back, I thrust my breasts out, and the slick folds of my pussy rubbing over the head of William's cock, teasing him. He groaned, and his hips moved, thrusting upward.

In this position, with the plug in my bottom, I was much tighter than usual. We both moaned as he entered me. He felt huge, trying to push inside of me as if there wasn't enough space for both him and the plug. Was this how it would feel when I was wedged between them? I wasn't sure I would be able to take it.

"Damn, you feel so good," William said as I worked myself up and down in small bounces, taking a little more of his cock inside each time I fell while he massaged my breasts. I barely felt the throbbing of my chastised bottom anymore, too focused on my growing pleasure.

"She looks so good, too," Clive said, pumping his cock as he walked up to us. He took my chin in his free hand, turning my head to give me a deep kiss as I sank onto William's cock.

My two wonderfully wicked husbands.

Clive released me and climbed on the bed behind me, and my whole body tingled in anticipation. This was it.

William pulled me down to him, his cock fully embedded in my pussy, kissing me as Clive eased the plug from my bottom. I sighed with momentary relief as my muscles were able to relax.

It wasn't to last, though. Almost as soon as the plug was out, Clive's cock was prodding at the stretched entrance, pushing it back open.

I moaned against William's lips at the intense sensations running through me.

Clive's hands rubbed over the sensitive cheeks of my reddened buttocks as his cock pushed between them. He was as thick as the thickest part of the plug, but the plug had been tapered, and the tight ring of my entrance had spent most of its time, firmly squeezing the notch between the plug's bulb and base. Now, it was being forced open around Clive's cock, fully stretching without relief, and my muscles spasmed.

I was far too full, yet I didn't want him to stop. I wanted to feel both of them inside me, filling me—claiming me.

My bottom burned inside and out as Clive's cock slid deeper, making me writhe between him and William. The muffled noises I made against William's lips were half-pleasure, half-pain—the burning discomfort of

Clive's cock impaling me warring with the tingling bliss of being so wonderfully *full*.

"She's so damn tight," Clive said through gritted teeth, pulling back, then thrusting in. The dragging motion made me moan again, my pussy and ass clamping down around them both.

William shifted beneath me, his cock retreating, then Clive slammed home, and I cried out. He was fully in my ass, and William's cock was thrusting back in, filling me completely. It was exquisite erotic agony, leaving me dangling on the thin line of pleasure and pain until I couldn't tell which was which.

Then they began to move. Clive's cock retreated, then thrust back in as William pulled out.

I was caught between them, swept away by the carnal rhythm of their thrusts. Clive's body slapped against mine, reigniting the burn in my chastened cheeks, while William's body heaved beneath me, rubbing against my clit with every thrust. The sensations were too raw, too sinful, too intense to be borne, yet I had no choice but to bear them.

I screamed my ecstasy between them as they moved harder and faster, overpowering me completely. I was caught in the maelstrom of their passion, ravaged by it, and it swept me away until we were all crying out together in abject rapture. They buried themselves inside me, pulsing, their hard bodies around me, and emptied their bliss into me.

Happiness surged, despite how sore I knew I was

going to be tomorrow. I rested my cheek against William's chest and felt Clive rest his against my back as their cocks shrank inside me.

They were the best thing that had ever happened to me, and I was never letting them go.

I might be a harlot, but I was *their* harlot. Forever.

EPILOGUE

HUMMING HAPPILY UNDER MY BREATH, my smile broadened when I saw my husbands coming for me. Sitting on one of the benches at the town picnic while they waited on me hand and foot amused me so. My gruff Clive and my sweet William had both turned especially protective ever since I began increasing.

"I brought you lemonade." Clive placed the glass down in front of me before claiming the seat on my right.

"And I brought you pie." The winning smile that went with William's offering was a sharp contrast to Clive's grumpy face and yet I loved each of their expressions equally, though for different reasons.

"Thank you both," I said primly, beaming at each of them in turn.

Other ladies and their husbands were in similar circumstances all around, children were running under foot, and there was a general air of happiness surrounding the whole town. I still could not believe how lucky I was. When I came to Bridgewater, all I had truly wanted was to be safe, yet here I was in love and well loved in turn, and with our first child on the way.

Over the past few months, I had even begun to make some friends about town. I waved to Maddy and her husbands as they walked by – we had bonded over being mail order brides. All of the women were so friendly and, just like my husbands, none of them cared about my past. I had found everything I wanted and so much more.

There is something very special about Bridgewater. Maybe it's the mountain air, maybe it's the town itself, or maybe it's just these wonderful men. All I know is, I never want to leave.

**BRIDGEWATER
BRIDES**

Want more Bridgewater Brides?
See the full list of books in the world:
http://bridgewaterbrides.com/books/

Be sure to sign up for the world newsletter to stay up to
date on new releases:
http://bridgewaterbrides.com/mailing-list/

ABOUT THE AUTHOR

About me? Right... I'm a writer, I should be able to do that, right?

I'm happily married, and I like tater tots, small fuzzy animals, naming my plants, hiking, reading, writing, sexy time, naked time, shirtless o'clock, anything sparkly or shiny, and weirding people out with my OCD food habits.

I believe in Happy Endings. And fairies. And Santa Claus. Because without a little magic, what's the point of living?

I write because I must. I live in several different worlds at any given moment. And I wouldn't have it any other way.

Want to know more about my other books and stories? Sign up for my newsletter for free stories or come visit my website to check out my books.

You can also come hang out with me on Facebook in my private Facebook group!

Thank you so much for reading, I hope you enjoyed the story... and don't forget, the best thing you can do in return for any author is to leave them feedback!

Stay sassy.

OTHER TITLES BY GOLDEN ANGEL

Standalone Romances

Mated on Hades

Marriage Training

Dirty Heroes

The Lady

Domestic Discipline Quartet

Birching His Bride

Dealing With Discipline

Punishing His Ward

Claiming His Wife

Bridal Discipline Series

Philip's Rules

Undisciplined (Book 1.5)

Gabrielle's Discipline

Lydia's Penance

Benedict's Commands

Arabella's Taming

Deception and Discipline

A Season for Treason

Venus Rising Quartet

The Venus School

Venus Aspiring

Venus Desiring

Venus Transcendent

Venus Wedding

Stronghold Series

Stronghold

Taming the Tease

On His Knees (book 2.5)

Mastering Lexie

Pieces of Stronghold (book 3.5)

Breaking the Chain

Bound to the Past

Stripping the Sub

Tempting the Domme

Hardcore Vanilla

Steamy Stocking Stuffers

Black Light

Defended

Black Light Roulette: War

Masters of the Castle

Masters of the Castle: Witness Protection Program Box Set

Tsenturion Masters with Lee Savino

Alien Captive

Alien Tribute

Big Bad Bunnies Series

Chasing His Bunny

Chasing His Squirrel

Chasing His Puma

Chasing His Polar Bear

Chasing His Honey Badger

Chasing Her Lion

Night of the Wild Stags – A standalone Reverse Harem romance set in the Big Bad Bunnies World

Poker Loser Trilogy

Forced Bet

Back in the Game

Winning Hand

Poker Loser Trilogy Bundle (3 books in 1!)

9 781393 155768